Shmooky

And Other
Post-Mid-Life Confessions

David Sierra

Alan, Karen & Amy
Thank you for your
friendship.
Love,
David 11/28/09

Eloquent Books
New York, New York

Eloquent Books
An imprint of AEG Publishing Group
845 Third Avenue, 6th Floor—6016
New York, NY 10022
http://www.eloquentbooks.com

ISBN: 978-1-60860-773-0

Book Designer: Bruce Salender

Printed in the United States of America

Dedication

To my mother, Carolyn Paladino Sierra.
Your prayers and support helped me through my darkest days.

Contents

Acknowledgements

It took me close to a year to write this short novel and it has been an unforgettable experience. Many sleepless nights were spent agonizing over every word and line with the knowledge that I would soon have to report with a clear head to my day job as a trial lawyer. There were many moments of frustration and despair both in the writing and finding a publisher willing to give a break to a first-time novelist. I could not have done it without the support of my family and friends. My seventy-nine-year-old mother spent countless hours on the phone giving me the strength to press on when I thought of giving up. My son, David, perhaps my toughest critic, read the initial manuscript in one sitting and stunned me not only with his praise but also with suggestions that I later incorporated into the final story. My daughter, Robyn, did the first editing and waded through my countless punctuation and grammatical errors while trying not to laugh too hard. I also want to thank my four best friends, Mike Fiorello, Alan Wysocki, George Puig, and Rey Gomez; my brothers, Marc, Donn and Kevin; my sister, Leslie; and my cousin, John Bishop, who have kept me laughing for decades and provided the inspiration for many of the stories in this novel. Special thanks to my first non-family reader, Kathleen Davies, who convinced me that my work was worthy of publication at a time when I was having my deepest doubts; and Jasmine Molinet and Amy Simo for their help in the conception of the cover design. There are too many others to name individually but I thank all of you for your friendship and support. I also want to thank my publisher, Eloquent Books, for taking a chance and publishing my first novel.

1. Both Sides Now

I've looked at love from both sides now
From give and take, and still somehow
It's love's illusions I recall
I really don't know love at all
        —Joni Mitchell
        —As performed by Judy Collins

No longer young, but not yet old, a man of fifty possesses a level of self-assurance only a half century of living can provide. The wit, polish, and worldly charm so conspicuously absent in a man in his twenties or thirties are now at his command. It should be the start of a man's glorious decade when all of the long years spent building a career, making connections, reading and traveling come together to form the perfect embodiment of masculine success: a James Bond in the form of a venerable Roger Moore, not the current stand-in. I expected nothing less on May 16, 1981, the day I entered the professional world. The crowd of well-wishers cheered, hugged, and kissed us as we made our way down the steps of the Georgetown University Chapel and into a waiting limousine. I felt the invincibility of youth, victoriously clutching my law school diploma in one hand, as my beautiful bride held the other. It seemed at the time that nothing could stop us. We were off to the promised land of affluence, position, and wealth on that gloriously warm, spring day in the nation's capital.

My name is Sam Russo, and I am the happy-go-lucky, class skipping, Scotch-swilling scholar who met the beautiful and passionately ambitious Jennifer McNamara, early in my first year of law school. We stayed together three tumultuous years, with our classmates dubbing us the "odd couple." She worked furiously to maintain her position in the top five of our class, while I fought off all challengers who tried to remove my stranglehold on the bottom. Jen could have worked anywhere, and despite her life-long dream of practicing at the pinnacle, turned down numerous offers from New York law firms to follow me deep into the provinces to settle in Orlando.

When we moved here in 1981, Disney World had been open for less than ten years, and the growth rate was staggering. It would still be another two decades before Orlando could even pretend to be a major city. However, the lack of an entrenched establishment made it the perfect place for two young, ambitious professionals to start their careers and move to the top much faster than could be expected in long-established business centers. By the time Jen and I were in our mid-thirties, we were the envy of our friends and colleagues, bringing in close to $300,000 per year. We had a home in fashionable Winter Park, and an ocean-front condo on New Smyrna Beach. Our only child, Alexa, was born in 1986 and quickly developed into the perfect daughter. She was brilliant, beautiful, athletic, and a natural leader. She excelled in everything despite the fact that her parents were usually too busy to give her the attention she deserved.

What could possibly go wrong? Just about everything. What appeared to be rising stardom as a trial lawyer floundered into mediocrity when I was forty, due to a combative and loveless marriage, general dissatisfaction with the legal profession, and a love of golf, football betting, and, most of all, booze. It was on the very day that my twenty-seven-year marriage to Jen mercifully came to an end that fate intervened to offer me just the slightest hope of redemption.

The malignancy of my old life was extracted without the courtesy of anesthesia on the Friday before Labor Day weekend 2008. For the next four months, my existence would be as precarious as a lit novena candle in a drafty church. A single flame would flicker desperately only to end in a faint trail of smoke, the weak, fading light put out by my own hand. I now stand alone in my kitchen staring into an open drawer. It is December 29, 2008, and although I have learned to hate the holidays, I just had a joyous Christmas for the first time in a decade. The coming New Year with its fresh start and promise of "change you can believe in" should be eagerly anticipated. Instead, I feel nothing but dense, unyielding pain—pain without hope—the kind of pain that causes a man to choose amputation over keeping the offending limb.

To understand how I got here would require volumes of tedious analysis, so let's just say the serious boozing started during my high school years in Pittsburgh. I was the son of a prominent tax lawyer and a strict but doting mother. It was 1970 and the counter-culture was thriving, with Nixon still looking for a way to get out of Vietnam while, at the same time, continuing to escalate the violence. Drug use and resistance to the war became synonymous, and although I wasn't crazy about the war, I had no desire to experiment with drugs.

I was a decent athlete but certainly not of the caliber to make a living at it. I worked-out hard and had no use for the potheads, freaks, long-haired pukes and other assorted losers that sullied the hallways of my high school. When it came to mind alteration, my experience would remain limited to beer, and while the experts debated the long-term effects of drug use in the late 1960s and early 1970s, the only on-going debate I was concerned about was whether Lite beer tasted great or was less filling.

Everything changed in college at Penn State. Unlike high school, where the potheads were in the minority and easily identified, in college I now found that I was a minority of one. It made me reassess the whole issue if I wanted to have a social life. I was literally the only non-imbiber at every party I went to early in my freshman year. New friends and acquaintances also looked at me with suspicion because I didn't burn it, as if I were some kind of narc. I never could handle outcast status. My opinion of the potheads also changed. Many didn't fit the stereotype I had held for years. These kids came from professional backgrounds, studied hard and were ambitious. The only thing that distinguished them from their parents was that pot was substituted for or, in most cases, added to liquor. It also concerned me that if I ever wanted to get laid again, I would need to start getting stoned. Pronto.

The pressure was unbearable, and two months into my freshman year, I started down the path of self-annihilation. I lived in a dormitory suite with three stoners: my roommate, Al Goldstein, and two suitemates, Han Chin and Adi Byu. It got so bad that in the winter, I didn't even bother going to class for weeks on end. We taped aluminum foil over our dorm room windows so that it was impossible to determine the time of day or what the weather was like outside. We would stay up until three or four in the morning, listening to Led Zeppelin, Black Sabbath, The Moody Blues and Pink Floyd, while frying our brains to the max.

Since childhood, I had a tendency to become obsessed with novelties, and pot smoking would be no exception. I was fascinated with the whole lifestyle and spent hours reading *High Times* and studying the seemingly limitless variety of bongs, pipes and other paraphernalia. I could identify the country of origin of weed and cultivated my own, right in the dorm room. It wasn't very good, but it helped us get through the dreaded dry periods that threw the rest of the campus into a panic.

Hours were spent in the quest of the perfect joint. Seeds and stems were carefully removed prior to the slow, deliberate ritual of rolling a joint that was firm and free of air pockets, yet not so tight that it would inhibit a good drag. Saving the roaches was all important as the dregs of the spent joint contained weed that was far more powerful than its virgin form. These dark, oily remnants would be re-rolled into powerful new joints dubbed by Al as "Hall of Famers," and would be saved for special occasions such as birthdays and the Super Bowl.

My parents were clueless. I remember the time my father made a surprise visit from Pittsburgh to State College one fall afternoon. He called me from the dormitory lobby and asked to come up to see my room. My suitemates scattered like cockroaches leaving me to deal with the sudden catastrophe. I tried to straighten things up, sprayed ozone in the air and laid out a couple of open books to make it look like I was hard at work. That took a few frantic minutes as I had forgotten where I had put them. Unfortunately, my dorm room, as well as the rest of the floor, smelled like an opium den.

I was still buzzed when I took the elevator down to meet him. He hugged and kissed me, but I could tell he was alarmed by my appearance. I had let my hair and beard grow and had also put on about forty pounds, which completely obscured the muscle tone I was so proud to possess in high school. That's the other thing about pot: it gives you the munchies. So after an all-night blow-out, the first thing you wanted when you woke up at 3:00 p.m. the next day was a pizza. I am not talking about a slice or two. I am talking about a whole pizza, washed down by a pitcher of beer, day after wasted day.

As soon as the elevator doors opened to my floor, the pungent aroma of marijuana was all pervasive. "What is that smell?" he asked, cringing in disgust. I looked right at him with a straight face and said, "What smell?" He didn't figure it out that day and left campus after about an hour without much in the way of disapproval.

The truth is I really didn't care what he was thinking as he certainly wasn't one to practice temperance. How could he disapprove? To him, getting trashed was a Jack Daniels Manhattan, straight up, with a maraschino cherry, in a ridiculous froufrou glass. He would knock back five or six of those before dinner as far back as I can remember. After dinner, he would start with the cognac. I sometimes wondered how he was able to run a successful law practice with these habits. I learned later in my own career that it can be done. It just takes practice, perseverance and Alka-Seltzer just before bedtime. So who was he to pass judgment on me?

Han Chin had getting stoned down to a science. He was a physics major from California, born in Taiwan, who used his genius to invent the ultimate communal bong. He apparently watched a lot of *Quick Draw McGraw* cartoons when he was growing up, because he named his invention El Kabong. It actually resembled one of those Arab smoking pipes, a hookah, with many short pipes leading into a receptacle that then fed into a long, flexible pipe with a gas mask at its end. Three or four guys could take massive hits at one time and then blow their used smoke back into the receptacle. Then, the asshole wearing the gas mask would inhale the toxic fumes through the long pipe. Theoretically, the guy wearing the gas mask could get completely wasted with just one inhalation.

We had one of our frequent floor parties on a night in which Pittsburgh was playing Philadelphia on Monday Night Football. Everyone had their doors open, and the televisions were blaring with the voice of Howard Cosell exalting over the thrill of watching a Pennsylvania intrastate grudge match. The floor was evenly divided between Eagles and Steelers fans, and at first everyone got along. As the game, drinking, and pot smoking wore on, a giant wet toilet paper fight ensued with guys throwing huge wet globs into each other's faces at point blank range. As the future leaders of America, we all had a blast.

I had a brief scare during the melee when some dip-shit threw an M-80 smoke bomb into our room. Seeing the word smoke, I took my time throwing it back only to have the mislabeled bomb blow-up in my face, temporarily blinding me. Once I got over the shock, and my sight returned, we all laughed our asses off before getting serious about getting stoned.

I hadn't tried El Kabong yet, but Han Chin warned me to take only a moderate-size hit. I thought, *Hey, he is Chinese; of course he can't hold his pot like an American.* So I blew out every last bit of oxygen from my lungs out of fear I would not get the maximum effect. I then inhaled as deeply as I could and held it in until my face turned beet-red before blowing it all out. I coughed uncontrollably like an eighty-year-old chain-smoker, but at first, it didn't feel like much, so I took off the gas mask and flexed my biceps in triumph. At that point, it hit me like a George Foreman punch in the nose, and the entire room started spinning. I then fell into an end table, breaking the lamp, and putting the entire room into hysterics. Unfortunately, there was a glass ashtray on the end table, which became lodged up my ass, requiring several stitches following extrication. It was an embarrassing emergency room visit, but I still didn't think I had a problem.

While at Penn State, I also developed an obsession with sports betting. I had considerable knowledge of my own, but my roommate, Al, a hysterically funny New Jersey Jewish boy, had a mind for the stuff like a walking computer. Even when we were stoned, I could give him the weekend's match-ups, and he could predict the line within a half point. We pooled our resources and kicked our bookie's ass week after week. Unlike our friends, we never needed a part-time job. We made enough cash to eat and drink well, smoke a boat-load of pot and take the occasional road-trip to Pittsburgh or Philly to catch a football or basketball game. Along with drinking, betting was a vice I would enjoy for the rest of my life. But I really only did it for fun and a little additional income. To Al, it was his life, and he moved to Nevada after graduation. By the time he was thirty-five, he was one of the leading line-makers in Vegas.

The fourth man in our suite was a Nigerian, Adi Byu, who claimed to be a direct descendant of a royal bloodline that once ruled his tribe. He was immediately dubbed "Shaka" and was the only guy on the floor who didn't get the joke. Adi also loved getting low but could be obnoxious when insisting African pot was far superior to anything grown in the western hemisphere. We thought it was a dubious claim and told him so. This usually resulted in him threatening to have us impaled. I have to admit that he did know his shit. Through his close associations with the black American drug dealers on campus, he always had superb weed. He also had one of those peculiar African accents, and Al would constantly torment him by doing a perfect impression of his voice when singing, "How sweet it is to be Adi Byu" to the tune of a James Taylor song that was popular at the time.

My report card for the first year was the clincher. I was on academic probation with a 1.9 GPA. I had exactly one more chance to bring it over a 2.0, or I would be out on my newly-scarred ass. My father called, expressing his disappointment. He was initially very solemn when he warned me that I had only one more chance. If I did not get serious, he was going to bring me back to Pittsburgh where I could find a job or go to community college. Another alternative he suggested was to go into the military, which in 1975, was about as appealing as committing yourself to a four-year sentence in a North Korean prison camp. By the end of the conversation, he could not hide his anger. "Listen, Samuel, listen to me carefully. I am not going to continue to invest in failure. I am tired of this horseshit. I love you. Goodbye." Holy shit! He sounds serious this time.

After a lot of soul-searching, I finally started to realize that I could study hard during the week and still blow my brains out on the weekends. I was desperate for his approval and told him that I had decided I wanted to go to law school. He laughed, and I got pissed-off. He said, "Prove it to me. Until then, I am going to laugh all I want, Asshole!" If I can give any advice other than never take a bong hit near a glass ash tray, it is never make a career move to please someone else. It was a decision I would regret for the next thirty years.

My father seemed to enjoy ridiculing me. I knew he loved me, and this was only his awkward way of trying to motivate me. When he got my next report card and saw the 3.75 GPA and a position on the Dean's list, he knew I was serious. He gave me every bit of his backing, and by 1978, I managed to bring my GPA up to the point where I was able to get into Georgetown law school.

In law school, the pot party stopped—not because I wanted it to, but because I couldn't find anyone to do it with. My classmates were all incredibly ambitious and did not want to take the chance of having a drug bust on their record. That is when I decided to devote all of my spare time after studies to becoming an alcoholic. I experimented for months trying to find the drink that would get me the most fucked-up without putting me on the bathroom floor. It wasn't easy, and I spent many weekend nights sleeping in the bathtub throwing-up on myself. I initially settled on Tennessee sour mash whiskey, and the joke around school was that while everyone was working toward earning a JD, a Juris Doctor, mine was a degree in Jack Daniels. After a few embarrassing black-outs, I switched to Scotch, and at last, the long quest had ended. I became a Scotch-and-water man and that I would remain.

Jennifer McNamara didn't need to experiment. She was from a wealthy, Baltimore family and arrived at Georgetown knowing exactly what she wanted out of life. She was determined to finish in the top five of our class and then get a job in a prominent New York firm at the highest salary offered to a rookie lawyer in the country. At that time, it was about $90,000 a year. Not bad for someone with no experience. By comparison, I started out working for an insurance company at a yearly salary of $18,000 and was grateful. She desired every piece of the pie including the home, car, clothes, jewelry, vacations, and, of course, a multiple six-figure income. All of this was supposed to happen within her first five years of graduation.

I looked at money as a necessity but wasn't driven by it. Give me a decent car that started reliably, a roof over my head in a neighborhood where I wouldn't get shot, a wet-bar with plenty of ice and Johnny Walker Red and a comfortable recliner in front of a color TV, and I would be satisfied. Throw in golf twice a month, an occasional pair of NFL or NBA tickets and an up-grade to Johnny Walker Black, and I would be in heaven.

You may wonder how we ever hooked up. It had everything to do with sex. She was a virgin when she started college at Princeton and immediately found a guy who was incredibly good-looking, intelligent, and rich, but had no idea what to do with his johnson unless he was holding it in his right hand. She fucked this guy for four years without once having an orgasm. I learned all of these interesting facts about her ex-beau the first night we met.

A couple of weeks into our first semester, the school put on a "Let's get to know each other" dance for the first year class. Jen, not having a clue how to hold her liquor, got trashed and asked me if I would walk her back to her dormitory. I reluctantly agreed to leave the dance because I was intrigued and wondered what made this peculiar girl tick.

As we walked, she would not shut up. I started to wonder why in the hell I had left with this obnoxious, self-absorbed bitch. Fortunately it was a short walk, and I thought I could be back at the dance in less than fifteen minutes once I dumped her.

"Don't you just love law school?" she asked.

"Uh, I don't know yet. Based on the amount of work that has been assigned so far, I am beginning to think I made a mistake coming here."

"But don't you think our professors are brilliant?"

"Actually, I think our Property professor is a flaming, self-loathing homosexual, our Criminal Law professor is a bleeding heart, knee-jerk liberal who wants to unleash vicious criminals on society in the name of human rights, and our Constitutional Law professor is a card carrying communist who would scrap the U.S. Constitution in a heart-beat if he could. Other than that, yeah, they are fucking brilliant." I was tired of the brief conversation and relieved when we reached her dorm.

"Are you a bad boy?" she asked as we stood at the front doorway.

"Excuse me?" I politely said, even though I was getting the feeling something, other than my johnson, was up.

"You know, a 'bad boy,'" she persisted.

"I am not sure what you mean; please explain."

"Okay, I think you barely qualified to get in to this school. I also think you are a hard-core boozer, and you did a lot of drugs in college. I think you are the type of guy who likes to go to strip clubs and get drunk and rowdy at football games. Am I close?"

"Close? I am beginning to think you have had me under surveillance for the last four years. So what is your point?" I asked with mild annoyance.

"Oh, I don't know. Do you want to come in for a little while? My roommate won't be back until late."

I stood there for a moment and thought, *I don't like her*. I had concluded that she was a stuck-up, rich bitch from the moment I laid eyes on her at law school initiation prior to the first day of class. However, I am not a complete moron. She was very cute, had an incredible ass and a beautifully proportioned rack. Of course I accepted the invitation and banged her with fervor all over the room. She was screaming so loud I thought for sure the resident assistant, who also happened to be a nun, would throw me out. We never heard from her. God knows what she was up to.

Jen's body had an almost celestial quality that no other woman through high school or college had come close to matching. Although there were many to reminisce about, all would ultimately fail miserably by all points of comparison. Her entire body did not have the slightest blemish, mole or faded freckle. The texture of her skin was so soft it made the 500-thread-count Egyptian cotton sheets we were fucking on feel like a potato sack. She had the tan bikini lines of a woman who had spent the entire summer at her parents' Maryland beach house. Her silhouette against the dormitory window left me in a constant state of arousal, even immediately following climax—three times in two hours. If only she could keep her mouth shut . . . for a moment.

"Is that thing always hard?" she asked with a look of serious concern, as if she thought I might be suffering from an affliction common to some sort of sexual deviant. When sheer exhaustion finally ended the romp, Jen told me all about her college boyfriend and her four years of frustration.

"That is why I picked you," she explained. "I thought that since you are a 'bad boy,' you would know how to do it."

"Why, thank you. I am very flattered that you hold me in such high esteem," I joked as I quickly got dressed and got the hell out of there.

As I walked back to the dance to see if there were any other alcoholics still hanging out, I had mixed emotions. On the one hand, the sex was awesome and by far, the best ever. But on the other, she was a major pain in the ass.

She woke up the next day and decided she was willing to overlook all of my failings and hang-out with me for the next three years. I guess she finally realized what it was about sex that had everyone all fired up. Deep down, I knew that getting further involved with her was a potentially serious mistake but went ahead with it anyway. It was one of those occasions when you say to yourself: go ahead, how bad could the time spent out of the sack possibly be? And then you regret it for the rest of your life.

Jen was the prettiest girl in the school, although I am using a law school rating scale. That means you have to put an asterisk next to the rating, because a seven in law school would rate no more than a five in the real world. What we considered a hottie at Georgetown Law would barely rate a sniff at Penn State. In any event, Jen was certainly a catch. She was a law school ten, which meant she was really about an 8.5. Not bad. She was not only beautiful but incredibly intelligent. Her only drawback was the fact that her mouth was as big as her brain. Our arguments would last for days, sometimes weeks. We would even argue during sex. She liked it that way. She wanted passion in addition to the physical release, and the only way she could get it out of me was to give me a swift kick in the nuts as I was taking off my shorts.

I don't think I ever really loved her. In retrospect, marriage was the next logical step, but I never actually sat down to seriously consider what it would be like to live with her for the rest of my life. We fought frequently in law school, but I failed to see the big picture. Besides, she did have some good qualities other than her beauty that had others in our class wondering what she ever saw in me. Unfortunately, she would spend the next twenty-five years trying to mold me into the guy she really wanted. I am a stubborn SOB, especially when my own precious principles are at stake and would not let her lead me down that road.

With our classmates frolicking in the bleacher seats, we were married at the Georgetown Chapel on graduation weekend. Jen's friends sat quietly through the solemn ceremony, while mine coughed "blow job" at every opportunity, mimicking the hearing to expel the Deltas scene in the movie, *Animal House.* Her parents looked on skeptically. I am sure they felt strongly that she could have done much better while mine were happy to see me finally grow up. My father was beside himself with joy. I was glad to see him so proud of me, since he would be dead of a heart attack ten years later at the ripe old age of fifty-nine. Not a good omen, as fear of my own impending death would be a huge factor in decisions I would later make in middle age.

After a wild reception at the Watergate hotel, we were off to Bermuda for a wonderful honeymoon of non-stop fuck-fests, interrupted by golf on some of the most beautiful courses in the world. When we returned, we packed the U-Haul, and headed to Orlando for what we thought would be a beautiful future living next door to Mickey and Minnie Mouse.

It didn't take long for things to deteriorate. Our marriage, during the remainder of the 1980s, closely resembled what was going on in the rest of the world at the time: an interminable, all-encompassing cold war with small brushfire guerrilla wars and police actions constantly flaring along the borders. In the '90s, with the cold war finally over, she changed tactics to coincide with the world's new brewing crisis and commenced training to become a terrorist. By the turn of the century, all she needed was a ski mask and her passport stamped: Afghanistan. I walked on eggshells around her, hiding my booze, only calling my friends when she was out shopping and having to sneak off to play golf. It was ridiculous, and by 2006, I had had enough.

2. It Ain't Me Babe

You say you're looking for someone
Never weak but always strong
To protect you and defend you
Whether you are right or wrong
Someone to open each and every door
But it ain't me babe
No, no, no it sure ain't me babe
It ain't me you're looking for, babe
*   —Bob Dylan*
*   —As performed by The Turtles*

"Equal Justice Under the Law." These inspirational words are inscribed over The Seal of The Great State of Florida in every courtroom at the Orange County courthouse in downtown Orlando. I was looking up at those words as the gavel fell, and the Judge proclaimed, "So ordered!" as the abrupt bang still echoed in my ears. Hearing the roar of approval from the other side of the courtroom, I stood up wanting to plead, "Wait!" but stood silently as my lawyer tugged on my arm to coax me to sit back down. It was now confirmed in the form of a Final Judgment that along with professional stagnation, drinking, gambling and a mid-life crisis every other year, I was now financially ruined. I ran out of the courtroom with both lawyers frantically trying to follow me. As a twenty-seven-year member of the Bar, I knew both of them well, and at that time, even considered Jen's lawyer to be a friend. They both pursued me as Jen, her boyfriend, family and friends remained celebrating in the courtroom.

Even by the low standards of our profession, Jen's behavior was despicable. If it had been a football game, she would have been flagged with a fifteen yard, unsportsmanlike conduct penalty for excessive celebration. This brain-dead judge didn't say a word and actually seemed amused by the spectacle. The only thing I could think of at that moment was what the great professional wrestling commentator, Gordon Solie, would likely have said in his deadpan delivery: "Let's take a commercial break while order is restored."

My attorney, Jim Richardson, got to me before I reached the elevator. He was a fat, unkempt slob who used his tie to wipe the sweat off his brow in the unbearable humidity that is Orlando in early September. He knew his way around the courthouse and was also expensive at $400 per hour, but considering the forces arrayed against me, I thought at the time I retained him that he was worth it. As it turned out, I couldn't have done any worse representing myself, and he chased me down with the guilty face of a loser.

"Sam, this is BS. I really think we should consider an appeal."

"For what?" I snapped. "To run up more attorneys' fees? No thanks."

The elevator door opened, and Jim quickly said, "At least think about it," as he rushed inside. He seemed relieved when I did not join him as he knew I was about to explode. I didn't get in with Jim because Jen's lawyer, Jack Spurlock, grabbed my arm.

Jack was a good ole boy with a keen sense of justice. As I pushed the down button again, I thought, *I really have nothing personal against him other than the fact that he took Jen's case.*

He is the top divorce lawyer in town. Doesn't he have enough other shit to keep him busy?

"Sam, I am really sorry about all of this. You know that I am just doing my job. I wanted to, but Jen would not let me let up on you. She really wants to see you destroyed."

"I always manage to bring out the very best in people," I quipped. "Look, Jack, there is no need for you to apologize. I understand why she is so happy but the high fives and doing 'The Bump,' the frigging Bump! Don't you think that's a bit much?"

"It actually could have been worse," Jack replied defensively. "You were awarded the downtown condo."

"Awarded? Gee thanks, Jack. If she had been given the condo, too, I would have been left with the choice of moving in with my mother or living in a dumpster. You are right; the result is absolutely fair. I work in this stinking profession for twenty-seven years, and she ends up with 80 percent of our net worth. Not to mention the $3,000 a month in rehabilitative alimony. Rehabilitative! What a joke. She graduated fifth in our law school class. I came in 143rd out of 144, and the guy who came in last was an affirmative action admission from east L.A. who could barely speak English."

"But Sam, she hasn't worked in three years," Jack pleaded.

"Give me a break. She could get a job today if she wanted one. But why should she when she can hang out with that douche-bag she is dating, and they can both party on my dime. I am the one who is going to need rehab. Credit and alcohol rehab. She is not even required to help pay for our only child to finish college. Basically, in addition to the condo, I get to keep my clothes, golf clubs, books, sports memorabilia and the contents of my wet-bar: the only items she wasn't interested in. Yeah, you are right. This is a very fair and just result."

Jack responded with an apologetic look, and said, "Sam, I am really sorry. Look, you can take your time paying my fees."

"Oh, thanks for reminding me that I also owe you about $25,000!" I exploded.

"Actually, I think it is closer to $40,000," Jack corrected me sheepishly.

Now I was really pissed and shouted, "Paying your wife's attorney's fees! That is like paying a terrorist to . . ."

Jack interrupted, "Sam, I think you are taking all of this very personally when it isn't personal. Come on, let me buy you lunch."

I glared at him while desperately trying not to punch him. Just then, the elevator door finally opened. I got in, looked back at Jack and said, "Jack, please don't take this personally, but *go fuck yourself!*"

Jack looked mortally wounded as the elevator door closed.

3. Here Comes My Baby

In the midnight moonlight, I'll
be walking a long and lonely mile
And every time I do,
I keep seeing this picture of you.
　　　　　　—*Cat Stevens*

I was enraged as I left the courthouse and stepped out into a steady drizzle. I couldn't bear to see Jen and her happy entourage emerge from the building, so I eschewed waiting around for the Lymmo bus and started walking down Orange Avenue without an umbrella. I thought, *Okay, there was my drinking, and gambling, and that ill-advised trip to Costa Rica, but is that a reason to want to completely destroy me? I am the father of her child for Christ's sake.* I needed a stiff Scotch and decided to head down to the Penalty Box, my favorite sports bar, several blocks away. It was about 98 degrees and combined with the 96 percent humidity created the perfect outdoor sauna that is late summer in Orlando. I didn't care. The cooling rain felt good and will help hide the perspiration stains on my shirt. Actually, summer in Florida officially starts on April 1 and doesn't end until November 1, which always made me wonder why people flock here from the temperate zone.

Although I had been determined to put an end to negative thinking, I couldn't help but conclude that at fifty-two, there was no way to avoid the conclusion that my life had become a complete train wreck. There was literally nothing I could point to as an enduring accomplishment. My marriage had ended in disaster, I was financially ruined and my career was stuck in neutral. In my mind, however, the most telling emotion was that I really didn't give a shit. Is this what they call a mid-life crisis? If so, the last ten years have either been one crisis after another, or just one long one. Feeling like shit had been the norm for so long, I was numb to it. Just then, a Lymmo bus passed, hitting a puddle and soaked me to mid-chest. I walked on, grateful that my face and hair were still relatively dry.

This was the culmination of a rough three years. My fiftieth birthday had hit me like I had just lost a Texas Death Match. There is no three-count. Someone has to leave on a stretcher with his face covered in blood: a crimson mask. My father never made it to sixty, and he arguably had much less stress than I have been forced to endure. My mother should be canonized as the patron saint of wives of alcoholics. Although she never drank, she learned how to make a superb Jack Daniels Manhattan and had one waiting for him as soon as he walked in the door. I rarely heard her nag him, and she was also very frugal. She always said, "If you have to use a credit card, you can't afford it." Needless to say, Jen hated her. I couldn't help but constantly ask myself: *If dad couldn't live out the decade with a saint like my mother, what could I realistically expect?*

It wasn't only the fear of impending death that hit me at fifty. Actually, there were days I would have welcomed death. What if there really are seventy-two virgins waiting for me? Hell, I would be satisfied with one. No, uh . . . two. If I only have a few more years, do I really want to spend the bulk of my remaining time in interminable arguments about three-year-old vehicular accidents with combative, sadistic verbal pugilists? I had concluded long ago that the life of a personal injury defense lawyer is a preposterous existence. Day after day, we stand toe-to-toe against self-righteous ambulance chasers in a hopelessly broken system, making only a fraction of what our esteemed brethren make representing their gold-digging hypochondriacs.

I "celebrated" my fiftieth with Alexa in Tallahassee during the fall of her sophomore year. Following that visit, I started having a recurring nightmare. It was always exactly the same. I am standing on Bobby Bowden field in nothing but a jock strap. The War Chant rises from the crowd and echoes in the vacant space in my skull that, pre-alcoholism, housed living tissue. It is the fourth quarter, and I am down three scores (Jen, work and debt). I have already burned all three time-outs, and all of my challenges ended with the official announcement: "After further review; you are screwed, Dude." Now the clock is running, and the raucous, hostile crowd is howling to see my head on the business end of Chief Osceola's flaming spear.

I told my psychiatrist, Dr. Wiener (pronounced wee-ner), about the dream in detail. He promptly informed me that I was "fucked-up" and glared at me when I asked him if that diagnosis is described in the DSM IV. Anyway, he doubled the dosage of my anti-depressants, which only served to put the whole mess into numbing slow motion, not to mention keeping my johnson as limp as pasta cooked well past *al dente*.

Our whole neurotic and depressed country is obsessed with mind-altering drugs. I am not talking about pot, with its side-effects of rapid weight gain, lethargy and if abused daily, termi-nal stupidity. I am referring to Xanax, Zoloft, Wellbutrin, and a host of other so-called anti-anxiety and anti-depressant medica-tions. Whatever happened to therapy such as "Stop whining," "Shut the fuck up, and get back to work" or "Oh, you don't like your job? Then quit and find another one, Asshole!"

In this politically correct world, we are all victims. No one wants to hear that they may be at least partially responsible for the interminable gloom that has overtaken their lives. It is much easier to blame the world and take a pill. I admit it all sounded good to me, but I still thought it might help to talk things over. However, during my first visit to Dr. Weiner, I quickly noticed that my pre-conceived Hollywood notions of psychiatry were completely erroneous. Yes, I sat on a couch, but it was immediately apparent that he had no interest in discussing and didn't give a rat's ass about the demons inhabiting my skull. If I dreaded the interminable trench warfare of personal injury litigation, I was suffering from anxiety, and Xanax was the cure. If I expressed disgust with the failure of my marriage or the lack of personal fulfillment at work, I was depressed, and there were numerous antidotes to choose from. He did mention something about side-effects, but I wasn't listening. Just give me the fucking drugs, Mofo!

Impotence and a complete loss of libido were the least of my problems. You have to appreciate a cure for depression that combines the side-effects of fatigue and drowsiness with insomnia. I would doze-off in meetings, behind my desk, at the movies, watching TV, reading, driving and even in the middle of a jury trial. Only a sharp kick in the ankle under the counsel's table by my partner returned me to the riveting courtroom drama concerning right-of-way and degenerative disc disease versus an acutely herniated nucleus pulposus. I could sleep anywhere except my bed. There I endured a torture far worse than waterboarding and would have gladly given the Chinese the plans for our future anti-anti-ballistic missile system in exchange for eight uninterrupted hours of sleep.

For months, I continued to tell myself: *This can't be. This cannot be all I have to look forward to.* Every morning, I wake up to another pointless, monotonous day of fender-benders, chiropractors and fake neck and back injuries, come home to hammer a few Scotches, fall asleep, and start the whole process over again the next morning. Men are not meant to live this way. We should be able to sleep off a hangover until 10:00 a.m. and then have our breakfast served to us in the clubhouse by college girls wearing cut-off jeans and bikini tops. We would tee-off at noon with those same girls now working the beer cart. After the round, it is back to the clubhouse for a few more beers before a hot shower and a massage—performed by a beer-cart girl. Dinner would be preceded by a two-hour nap (on a good day, accompanied by the beer-cart girl/massage therapist). Dinner is at 7 p.m. at a five-star steakhouse, lasts two hours and is topped-off by more Scotch and cigars. The evening is concluded with a trip to a men's club for fine entertainment until 2:00 a.m. This process is repeated the following day, and the day after that, and . . .

Some may ask if I would ever tire of this. My answer is: "No! Hell No!" If I need a change of scenery there is Pinehurst, N.C., the Robert Trent Jones tour in Alabama, Vegas, Tahoe, Hawaii, Costa Rica, and if I ever get tired of golf or gambling there is always Amsterdam.

Returning to the real world, I continued to lament the day's disaster as I walked in the rain down Orange Avenue. I couldn't even consider Alexa as an enduring accomplishment. She did it all on her own and was living in Tallahassee with her long-time boyfriend. Jen and I separated shortly after she graduated from high school, and I am sure she looked at us as people she had no intention of modeling her life after. Of course, what she doesn't yet understand is that no one enters a marriage knowing that failure down the road is all but certain. It just seems to happen unless both people are willing to put aside their egos and work to save it. Jen and I couldn't do that, and even if we could, we wouldn't. Neither of us wanted to give in and concede that the other had a point. It was a whole lot easier to just say "screw you" and move on.

So Alexa was living her life without frequent contact with me. We were not estranged. I spoke to her every couple of weeks, but I kept the subjects light and preferred to ask about her life rather than complain about mine. I loved her dearly and knew she loved me, but I didn't want her worrying about me, so it was better this way. I remember the day she was born. She had a birthmark of a heart on the back of her right shoulder. It was bright red and so perfectly shaped it worried me. Was it some sort of biblically prophetic mark signifying the coming Rapture and the imminent demise of lowly creatures like me? But it was my happiest day. I adored her every moment of her life and wanted to be a good daddy but knew I wasn't. It wasn't that I was bad. On the contrary, she was spoiled and over-indulged as cover for and as a diversion from her painfully aloof old man. In time the mark faded and disappeared, but my love for her never diminished. It was all the bullshit that distracted me. I regret it all and hope that it is not too late to fix things. My biggest concern now is how to pay for her wedding, which is set the week before Christmas, less than four months away.

In a crisis, you always tend to think about the few people who might actually care about your predicament. I felt fortunate that I had managed to stay in close contact with my best friend and college roommate. When I told Al I was getting divorced, his first reaction was, "What took you so long, you dumb *goyim?*" He hated Jen, and the feeling was mutual. He was my best man, but Jen would not "allow" me to see him. She hated Vegas, and the one time Al came east to visit was a complete disaster. Al got so tired of her ridicule that he challenged her to a "steel cage match." He asked me if I would mind if he gave her a head-butt off the top rope. I just grinned as I imagined him performing the move that was among the most daring in wrestling.

Sure, professional wrestling is fake, but it is the audacity of the spectacle while everyone knows it is fake that provides its entertainment value. When we were at Penn State, Al and I traveled to places like Erie, Hershey and Harrisburg to sit ring-side in grimy auditoriums to watch "The big cat" Ernie Ladd battle Bruno Samartino, as well as other notables like Killer Kowalski, Bronco Lubich, Aldo "Banana-nose" Bogni, "The Captain" Lou Albano and George "The Animal" Steele.

When I moved to Florida, the show was even more ridiculous and yet compelling, with the villains using geopolitical themes designed to bring the crowd to a murderous frenzy. There was the mad Soviet, Boris "The Great" Malenko, the neo-Nazi brothers, Kurt and Skull Von Stroheim, Abdullah "The Butcher" from The Sudan and the sadistic North Korean giant, Pak Song. The villains were all, at one time or another, pitted against the ultimate hero, Dusty Rhodes, the "American Dream." But what distinguished championship wrestling from Florida was its genius announcer, Gordon Solie, who developed a wrestling vernacular and delivery that, with the coming of ca-

31

ble television, spread to forty-eight states. Thirty years later, we continued to use "Gordon Solie-isms" in daily conversation. It was particularly appropriate for my law practice as there were always good guys and villains: "Pier 6 brawls," someone getting "Pearl Harbored," blows to the "solar plexus," illegal use of a "foreign object," tagging-up, submission holds, and the aforementioned Texas Death Match.

Anyway, Jen accepted the challenge but not the terms. She wanted a "loser-leave-town" match. I knew Al didn't have a chance. He left Orlando never to return. He hated the place anyway and wondered aloud how I could live in a "Mickey Mouse" town with no professional sports. To him the Magic didn't count, especially after Shaq Daddy left. He is wrong about that. It really is not so bad living here. Orlando is the biggest small town in America and the locals still desperately cling to that image while at the same time trying to convince anyone who will listen that it offers everything you would want in a world-class city. That may be an exaggeration but with each passing year the place has gotten a bit more interesting. Over the past quarter century, I have witnessed breathtaking growth but while we are proud that Orlando is now the twenty-seventh largest market no one is permitted to utter a discouraging word about the choking traffic, endless suburban sprawl, and rising crime rate. Those are problems they have in Miami and Tampa, not in "The City Beautiful." I have learned to appreciate this blind civic pride and have looked on in amusement when some jackass at a cocktail party blurts out something negative about this town and is met with looks of disapproval. Shh! Mickey will hear you.

I haven't seen him in over ten years, but Jen was not able to end our friendship. We talk once a week in the off-season, but during football season, we speak every day, sometimes as much as three to four times a day on the weekends. Al is so good at what he does; he feels that thorough technical analysis of the data, such as subtle movement of the line during the week preceding the game, injury reports, and weather conditions, along with consulting with coaches, scouts and sportswriters is not enough. As he would put it, "I also want to know what the average schmuck on the street is thinking." One day he told me, "You are that schmuck." I was cool with that.

When Jen and I separated, he suggested I move out to Vegas. I was so disillusioned with being a lawyer that I went to bartending school and thoroughly enjoyed the few hours a week I spent moonlighting. I have always had a fascination with the seemingly unlimited variety of alcoholic beverages and loved mixing drinks and talking to the colorful characters that hung around the bar. Al told me that there was unlimited work bartending in Vegas at income levels unheard of here. I would also be close to the action, which was one of the few things that got me going anymore. It was a thought that required serious consideration. So I did have some small reason to remain optimistic.

Eternal optimism was the one thing that had always saved me in the past, and this latest fiasco would be no exception. I thought, *Let's look at the bright side. The last ten years of my marriage had been absolutely miserable. It was a non-stop succession of fights and bickering, interrupted by long periods of silence. No wonder Alexa was so active in high school. Her home life sucked.* I also knew I would never marry again. Most of my married friends were miserable, and I could honestly say that, with maybe one exception, I would rather be dead than married to any of their wives.

As I approached central downtown, my mind wandered onto more joyous thoughts: *No more criticism. No more ridicule. No more incessant nagging. No more reminders that she could have married an orthopedic surgeon who loved her ass unconditionally. No more arguments over the remote control to the widescreen TV. No more of her changing the channel from FOX News to CNN. My mind raced with more delightful thoughts. How about no more nights watching the Home and Garden Network or the Food Channel (although, if I could duct tape her mouth, I wouldn't mind banging Rachel Ray over every inch of her Giallo Veneziano granite kitchen counter-tops). No more complaints about my drinking, gambling, snoring and farting. No more shitty but expensive vacations.* I could go on and on. Yes, despite being broke, maybe life was looking up.

I was soaking wet by the time I finally reached The Penalty Box. I sat down and wondered if there was anything on the menu I could still afford. I tried to think happy thoughts during the several block walk from the courthouse, but my competitive nature and sense of fair-play had taken a massive beating by the Court's ruling. Still seething, I only wanted to be left alone to analyze the betting line for the weekend's football games. It was Labor Day weekend, and although the pros would not start for another week, there were several interesting college match-ups on the card. Since I now had to pay Jen $3,000 a month indefinitely, I looked at sports betting with a new sense of urgency. As I was lost in thought, a young woman approached me.

"Excuse me sir, but I have not eaten in four days and would appreciate any help you could give me. Please."

"This is a restaurant not a bus station," I snapped. "They say that downtown has been declining, but this is fucking ridiculous."

Startled by the nasty, abrupt response, she replied with more than a hint of sarcasm, "Well, thanks for your kindness."

"No! You are not going to get away with that," I shouted.

"What?"

"Making me feel guilty. Making me feel like shit."

"If you feel like shit sir, maybe it is because you are—"

"Are what?" I interrupted.

"A piece of shit."

"Why you little bitch, or is it now pronounced bee-otch? Get the fuck—"

As the confrontation escalated, the manager and long-time betting enthusiast, Charlie Jackson, walked up and asked, "Is this woman bothering you, Sam?"

"Well, using the term 'woman' is a stretch don't you think, Charlie?" Charlie laughed as she looked as if she was about to cry.

"Miss, you must leave now or I am calling the police," warned Charlie.

I looked back at her as the emotion was building in her face. I then mocked her unmercifully, "There go the tears. I am so moved."

With her tears and rage barely under control, she shouted, "You're a bastard!"

"Look little girl, if you want to trade insults with me, be my guest because I will kick your skinny little ass. I am a personal injury lawyer. I insult people for a living and went to school for many long years to develop my skills. That's seven more years than you have—assuming you graduated from high school, which I doubt."

She ran out, and Charlie immediately changed the subject to football as if the ugly incident never happened. It was strange, but I did not feel exultant as I watched her hurriedly leave the restaurant through the front window. She appeared to be little more than five feet tall and one hundred pounds, wearing faded blue jeans with a large hole at the right knee, worn-out white sneakers, a blue T-shirt and a Cleveland Browns backpack tied around her waist. The real fashion statement was the Cleveland Indians baseball cap with her ponytail sticking out the back.

She was actually kind of cute in a trampy, tomboy way, and as she passed around the corner, I started to feel bad for being such a nasty bastard. I normally don't treat people that way and prided myself as being different from other lawyers who took their combative misery and inflicted it on the rest of the world. It was the stress of the divorce that had turned me into a bitter, impatient old man. I knew I had to put a stop to it before it consumed me.

4. *Crimson and Clover*

Now I don't hardly know her,
but I think I could love her
　　　　　—Tommy James and the Shondells

The whole incident did not sit well with me for the rest of the day. I felt an incredible desire to find her and apologize. After lunch, I walked around downtown to let off some steam and possibly find the victim of my vicious outburst. I checked all of the usual spots where the young counter-culture hung out, but she was nowhere to be found. In frustration, I walked back to my condo and absorbed the eerie silence as the door shut behind me.

I had been alone for almost three years but still had not completely adapted to the emptiness. During the first few months following our separation, the loneliness hit me like a life sentence in solitary confinement at a supermax prison. For twenty years, I came home from work to a house full of noise. There was always Jen's nagging, Alexa's TV or music, or Jen and Alexa arguing. Even when they were away, I could always count on a warm greeting from Emma (aka Enema), our Yorkie, with her adorable little face and sawed-off, half-inch tail wagging fu-

4. Crimson and Clover

riously. Many men stay in hateful, torturous marriages out of fear of this silence, but I had gradually learned to appreciate the peace and solitude as a respite from the madness that was my profession. For the first time in decades, I was able to read books rather than short magazine articles. Living downtown had also eliminated a tedious commute, further simplifying my existence. If I did need some noise, I could always turn on the TV or radio, or go downstairs. For the most part, I had adjusted well to my new life, but today, I just sat there in silent thought—not about the hundreds of thousands of dollars I had just lost but kicking myself for being such an ornery old bastard. I continued to flashback to the hurt I saw in the girl's eyes as I ridiculed her.

I drank six or eight Scotches before going to bed. The next morning, I woke up in my usual haze and put on ESPN's College Gameday. It was the first big weekend of the season, and normally, I could not wait to hear Lee Corso and company discuss the weekend's match-ups. I had nothing planned for the next three days but to watch seven football games and drink 1.75 liters of Johnny Walker Black. However, it was immediately apparent that this opening day would be different. I watched the show with listless indifference as I thought of how I had violated my own personal oath to avoid the deliberate infliction of pain.

Al called from Vegas at about 11:00 a.m. to give me a complete rundown of the upcoming action. He is involved with basketball and horse racing as well but nothing tops the football season. We waited seven months from the end of the last Super Bowl for this weekend, and he was so excited I could almost feel his breath coming through the phone. He immediately noticed my unusual lack of enthusiasm. "What the hell is your problem?" he demanded. I told him the whole story and was surprised when he didn't repeatedly interrupt me as was his custom.

"You know what it is" he said matter-of-factly.

"No. What?"

"You smelled some YP, and now you are kicking yourself."

"YP?" I asked curiously.

"Yeah, you know, young pussy."

I should have known. Al always liked to break things down to initials to save time conveying his betting releases, and he would use his system humorously when talking about other issues, especially sex. There was OP: old pussy, NP: new pussy, SC: sloppy culo (ass in Spanish), ST: sloppy tits, etc.

"You are a disgusting pig," I replied annoyingly.

"Oh, I am so sorry. You really liked this YP," he said mockingly.

"I don't know" I replied earnestly. "There was something about her, and I didn't realize it until after I had made her cry."

"You aren't known for being a hard-liner."

"I know. I can't believe how mean I was, but I had just gotten out of the final divorce hearing and was pissed-off. Now I feel terrible."

"If you don't snap out of this I am going to have to fly over there and come off the top rope to beat some sense into you," he threatened.

"Coming off the top rope" is wrestling vernacular. The move is usually performed as a final sadistic strike prior to pinning an opponent. When his foe is obviously beaten and is lying helpless on the canvas, the victorious grappler will climb the three ring ropes and stand on the turnbuckle. The crowd will then encourage him to jump on the limp body of the defeated wrestler as the final *coup de grace* before pinning him. It is usually performed as a flying elbow shot to the throat, but some acrobatic wrestlers will use the dreaded head-butt off the top rope—probably the most feared move in the sport.

I agreed to drop the subject, and we went on to discuss the weekend's card. Figuring my financial condition could not get any worse, I put more on the line than I ever had on a single weekend's games. Fortunately, Al was particularly sharp, and I made a killing, but even that could not shake me out of the deep funk I was in over this young and apparently homeless woman. Over the entire three-day weekend, I left my condo every few hours to walk around downtown in the blazing heat looking for her without success.

Al was worried and called again on Monday afternoon. I was in a semi-drunk haze and told him how much I was not looking forward to returning to the office the next morning.

"I know you have been obsessed with your divorce and that double-death case you have been telling me about, but don't you have any other interesting cases coming up?" he asked.

"Actually, I do have one that appears to be a sure trial this month. My truck driver had partially committed into his left turn before seeing an oncoming speeding motorcyclist. He was able to come to a complete stop with the front end of his cab partially obstructing the motorcycle's lane. The bike was coming so fast he T-boned the stopped cab."

"Was he ejaculated?" Al quipped.

"Yeah, and it must have been spectacular because witnesses say the kid somersaulted across three lanes of East Colonial before landing head first into a large U.S. Mailbox. Miraculously, he only broke his wrist and had a few other minor injuries. He was able to walk away, but his lawyer wants no less than $250,000 because his client 'could have been killed.' We offered him $50,000 at mediation."

"That may be a little light," Al replied.

"I agree. I thought we should pay him something extra for getting him airborne, but the company wouldn't go for it. There is nothing worse than being forced to go to trial during the football season. It ruins the whole weekend."

On Tuesday morning, I walked to the office knowing that the preparation for and distraction of the final divorce hearing had put me dangerously behind at work. I tried desperately to focus that morning but could not concentrate. I couldn't get her out of my mind, and at about 11:00 a.m., I left to walk around central downtown hoping to run into her. I was disappointed at the thought that she may have been just passing through. I couldn't understand why I cared, but when I passed the abandoned doorway and looked inside, I felt intense relief to see her baseball cap with Chief Wahoo grinning back at me. She had her head between her knees as if she was sick. I stood there until she noticed my presence and looked up. I smiled and said, "Hi." I immediately saw the look of recognition in her face, but her reaction was not what I had hoped.

"What do you want, you mean old bastard?" she said dismissively.

I was initially surprised by her attitude but knew I shouldn't have been. I had treated her far worse last Friday and clearly she had not forgotten it.

"I just wanted to say I am sorry, but I guess I deserve that. Well, anyway, I am very sorry."

She gave me a puzzled look but didn't say anything. I hesitated for a moment hoping for a response, but when none came I walked off dejectedly in the direction of Wall Street.

Wall Street in Orlando has no relation to the one in New York. It is a small thoroughfare in central downtown with a few bars, restaurants and outdoor cafes. It would be quaint if it did not also attract what I call the new-wave unemployed. They are mostly lower-middle-class white kids who show their disdain for society by covering their bodies with tattoos and their faces with metal spikes, studs and rings. If you thought the counter-culture of the late '60s and early '70s was unattractive, they were the beautiful people compared to this lot. These people disgusted me, especially the women. I couldn't help but cringe when I saw what would otherwise be an attractive female covered in tattoos and metal. Don't they have any respect for the beauty of their bodies?

When a hippie wanted to re-join the world he would take a shower, get a haircut, and put on some decent clothes. What are these assholes going to do when they wake up? Aren't those tattoos permanent? They are scarred for life. I didn't notice any metal or tattoos on this girl, and if all she had was a tramp-stamp above her ass, I could live with that. But she just told me to fuck-off, and I could not immediately move on from the disappointment.

As I walked slowly down Wall Street, I sensed that somebody was walking behind me. I turned around and there she was. I gave her a puzzled look and asked, "Hey, are you okay?"

I was shocked that her attitude had changed so dramatically from just a minute ago. She said pleadingly, "Can we start this over?"

"Okay," I replied. "I am Sam."

"Nice to meet you Sam. I am Sammie."

We both laughed at the coincidence, and I then said, "Are you still hungry? Because I'm going to lunch. Please join me."

"Sure," she replied, and we walked down to The TexMex Cantina and sat outside. It was a beautiful day, and the soft breeze and sunlight played upon her hair and eyes. This was the first time I really had a good look at her and quickly realized just how beautiful she was.

I started the conversation by stating, "First, I want to apologize. That man you met last week—that isn't me. I never talk to anyone that way. You can ask my secretary or any lawyer in town. I am really a nice guy. I swear."

She smiled and asked, "You're a lawyer? That's impressive."

"No, not really. Actually, I'd rather be known by my other profession."

"What's that?"

"I tend bar part-time, here downtown."

"Cool."

"I would like to say that I do it solely for personal enjoyment, but I also like the extra money. I am actually going to need it now."

"So what is wrong with that?"

"Nothing, I guess, which leads me into my excuse for my bad behavior."

"No need, Sam. I forgive you."

"Please, let me tell you anyway."

"Okay."

"You see, my divorce was final last Friday, and I pretty much lost everything I have ever worked for."

"That's awful. Couldn't you settle with her?"

"I tried. I offered her a 50-50 split and she laughed. I then offered her 60 percent, and that is when she hired the best divorce lawyer in town who used to be a friend of mine. She rejected all of my attempts to compromise, and last Friday, the judge awarded her close to 80 percent of our net worth, plus alimony. I had just left the courthouse when you came up to me, and I was still seething with anger. I took it out on you, and you didn't deserve that."

"I knew I was right," she replied.

"About what?"

"That you are a kind man. I don't typically approach people like I approached you. In fact, I never have, and I was scared shit-less. I looked at you for a few moments from outside through the window, and I could tell."

"How?"

"It's your eyes. You have kind eyes. They are very vivid and warm, but I am sure you hear that from all of the ladies."

"Oh yeah, my mother mentions it all the time."

"What about your ex? Don't tell me that wasn't her favorite part of you."

"Actually, in thirty years I don't know that she ever mentioned them. I think her favorite part of me was my ass, and I am not referring to it in a sensual or erotic way. I think she just liked kicking it around."

As we ate lunch, I found myself almost staring at her face. I was afraid she would notice, so I tried to look away as much as possible. I was truly captivated by her beauty but was not sure why, as she did not have the type of universal appeal that would bring the quick concurrence of most men. There was nothing exotic about her, but her flawless complexion and the symmetrical simplicity of her features had me mesmerized. Her doe-like brown eyes twinkled when she laughed, which alone was enough for me, but it would be hard to explain to anyone exactly what it is about her that has filled me with desire. She defies explanation as she is hopelessly unqualified to be a super model or Hollywood pin-up girl, and her petite, tom-boy body is almost completely devoid of curves. I couldn't help thinking that if she tried to earn a living as a table-top dancer, she would starve. But as difficult as it is to explain, the desire was real, and I was desperately trying to contain it as I watched with mild amusement as she stuffed each ketchup-soaked french fry into her lovely mouth, a scene I would normally find revolting. She ate ravenously, like it was her first decent meal in days, but was careful not to violate any rules of etiquette. She kept her mouth closed as she chewed and responded to my comments with nods of her head and laughing eyes that kept mine focused on hers as if controlled by some sort of tractor beam. The one thing I didn't get was the baseball cap, so as we were finishing lunch I asked, "So what's with Chief Wahoo?"

"Oh, I am kind of a sports nut, but I really love the Browns and the Indians. Baseball is my favorite. Do you watch baseball?"

"No, not much anymore. I am like Pete Rose. I never bet on baseball. Unless it is Penn State football or the Steelers, I can't watch any sport or even play golf unless I am down."

"Down?"

"Yeah, you know, have a bet on the outcome."

"You can't enjoy sports just for the excitement of the competition?"

"No, I am afraid not. To me, watching sports without betting is like watching people having sex with their clothes on."

"That's sick," she laughed.

"Hey! Are you sure you haven't met my ex-wife?" I asked smiling. "Because for a moment you sounded exactly like her. It is going to be difficult for us to be friends if you insist on impersonating her. That reminds me, let me see some ID."

"Why? Are you totally nuts?"

"No, I am serious. I have enough problems. If you aren't at least eighteen, I am going to have to say good bye. But it has been very nice talking to you."

"Okay, here," she said with mild annoyance as she handed me her driver's license.

"Ah, Ohio, the Buckeye State. When are you people going to learn how to play football?"

"Are you serious?" she replied incredulously.

43

"I am always dead serious when it comes to my betting record. Do you know how much money I have lost on Ohio State the past couple of years? And to get trounced by the Gators when those scumbags were a 7 point dog! I have to live with that shit around here."

"Well, like, you don't know jack shit dude. Many of the greatest players and coaches of all time are from Ohio. Haven't you ever heard of Paul Brown, Jim Brown, Otto Graham, Dante Lavelli, Gene Hickerson, Marion Motley, Leroy Kelly and Don Shula?"

"You forgot Lou Groza and Paul Warfield, but hey, I am impressed that you know any of those guys. But I am talking about this century, not the middle of the last one."

"Ohio is the birthplace of football," she retorted with irritation.

"Whenever anyone uses those 'birthplace' arguments that means they are getting their ass kicked and have nothing else to say."

She stuck her tongue out at me, which I took as notice that she was changing the subject.

"I can't believe you are so totally dumb. You have been looking at my date of birth and still can't figure out exactly how old I am." She giggled and said, "Let me explain in a way even you will understand. Take my birth date, and add twenty years. Then work from there. You see dummy, I am twenty and will be twenty-one in February."

"I will be the first to admit I suck at math. That is why I went to law school. But I am an expert at calculating numbers at intervals of 3, 4, 6 and 7 and totals of 37, 38, 40, 41, 43 and 44."

"So?"

"So, Miss Ohio, if you knew anything about football you would know those are football numbers."

"You are so totally brain-damaged, dude," she replied giggling.

Her laugh was so intoxicating. I didn't want the afternoon to end so I asked her, "Do you have time to go for a walk?"

"Sure. We could go down to the lake."

We walked out to Lake Eola Park. Lake Eola is really not much more than a large pond in the middle of downtown, but the natives are very proud of it. I saw the ridiculous wooden swan boats and said, "You know, I have lived here for over twenty-five years and have never had a ride on a swan. Let's do it."

"Okay, I would love to," she replied enthusiastically.

As we paddled out to the center of the lake, I found myself becoming more and more captivated by everything about her. *What the hell is wrong with me?* I thought. *I'm having so much fun. She's so cute and witty. I'm sure it is normal for a fifty-two-year-old man to feel this way with a twenty-year-old woman, but why does she seem to be so enthusiastic about hanging out with me? I would've thought that once we made peace and I fed her lunch, she would have run away as fast as she could. I feel so alive, so young. It is embarrassing. I hope no one I know sees me. Screw it. There are a few assholes who I would love running into about now.*

As we sat out in the middle of the lake, I started to wonder just what it was that got me: her sweet voice, her smile, and the way she laughs? I don't know. Was it the hole in her blue jeans? The beat-up and stained old backpack she uses as a purse? The baseball cap? Her complexion was so fresh and flawless without a hint of makeup. Her teeth were as white as snow, and when she took off her cap, her un-styled hair blew freely in the breeze, framing her face perfectly no matter how it fell.

But it was not just the physical attraction. There was no trace of demand in her voice. I was very familiar with that tone as my ex always used it, and even my daughter had a tendency to hit me with it when she started to lose patience with me.

I had no idea of her education level, but Sammie was bright, knowledgeable and funny. She did the same things I try to do for laughs: exaggerated facial expressions, different voices and a running commentary on life's absurdity. She seemed just ecstatic to be there with me—me—an old fart. So which one of us was the sick one? Or was it both of us?

All I knew was that I didn't want this to end. But it must. But why? We are both consenting adults. Right?

When the swan ride was over, we sat under a tree facing each other. We were only about a foot apart while we talked which was fine with me, but I feared that if she looked at me too closely, she would finally notice that I was over two-and-a-half times her age and deteriorating by the minute. Maybe she was far-sighted, because she didn't seem to notice. Or was it possible she has a thing for older men? I did inherit a few traits from my father other than a huge capacity for alcohol consumption and, like him, I felt myself rotting from the inside out. Although his overall look may have been flawed, his eyes were an unusual shade of blue that, combined with his dark hair and complexion, made him somewhat striking. He also didn't seem to age as rapidly as most men, which was amazing considering how much he abused himself. I remember people at his wake remarking how he made a superb-looking corpse.

She started to tell me about her life and how she got here.

"I am from Orrville, Ohio. It is an old manufacturing town about fifty miles south of Cleveland. Most of the factories closed years ago and my father lost his job when I was eight.

He couldn't handle unemployment and went into a deep depression. He would drink himself unconscious every night and died when I was thirteen. But he was a nice drunk. He was always wonderful to me, and I adored him. I was his only child, his little girl. He called me Shmooky."

"Shmooky?" I laughed.

"Yeah," she giggled.

"What is that from?"

"I have no idea. When I was a kid, I thought that was the way all drunken people talked. Anyway, after he died, I missed him terribly and made my mother suffer for it during my teenage years. You know, sex, drugs and rock 'n roll. She worked long hours as a nurse, and I took advantage of her absence. I love her but we just don't get along. I know she has been looking for me."

"You left without telling her where you were going?"

"Yes. I couldn't take it anymore," she replied defensively.

"You should at least tell her you are okay," I strongly suggested. "She is probably sick with worry."

"But I don't want to argue with her," she pleaded.

"You don't have to. Does she have e-mail?"

"Yes."

"My office is right across the lake. Let's go up, and you can use my computer."

"Oh, okay."

"If it was my daughter, I would be going nuts if she disappeared without a word."

"You have a daughter?"

"Yes, in fact she's just a year older than you. She is up in Tallahassee and is starting her last year at Florida State."

"What's her name?"

"Alexa. She is the love of my life. Now that I'm divorced, she is all I have."

"You have me now, Shmooky," she said in a tender, caring voice. I looked into her eyes. *Is she serious?* I wondered.

"Hey, I thought you were Shmooky."

"Well, now you are Shmooky, too," she giggled sweetly.

As we walked to my building, she took my hand. Her palm and fingers felt so soft and small. For some crazy reason, it felt right. It was a little awkward, but I did not want to let her go. Other people strolling around the park walked by and stared at us, some disapprovingly. For those, I reserved my unmistakable look of *fuck you*!

She held on and didn't let go until the elevator opened on my floor. As we walked through the front door, I could see that the feeble mind of our receptionist was, for once, working overtime. This was a lady who, before voicemail, would routinely leave you a written phone message with only six numbers.

"I am sorry, sir, but you know that the missing number must be a number from 0-9."

"Gee, you think? So I'm supposed to make as many as ten calls until I find the right number? Brilliant!"

A few minutes after one of those confrontations, I would receive a warning e-mail from the office manager, aka Mother Superior, instructing me to stop abusing the receptionist; I am creating a hostile work environment. This is the state of corporate America.

Gossip traveled in my office at speeds our current technology is unable to calculate. I knew that once "The Mole" was aware of Shmooky's presence, it would be around the office in a nanosecond. That prediction was a lock, and within five minutes of our arrival all twenty-five office employees managed to find a reason to stop at my office door to check out my new friend. It didn't take Shmooky long to figure out she was sitting in a fishbowl.

"Your co-workers are a little weird," she said with mild concern.

"Just a little?" I asked.

"So this is what a law firm looks like. What a beautiful view," she said as she gazed out at the lake. "You must love it here."

"Actually, no," I replied. "This is my golden cage, and I would give anything to be able to get out of here. I am sick of handling accident cases. They are all the same, and the thought of doing this for another ten years is frigging unbearable."

As she gave me a look of astonishment, I explained, "I do have one decent case. It involves an 18-wheel tractor trailer and two teenagers in one of those new "Smart" cars. I represent the truck driver who was trying to make a right turn onto an I-4 entrance ramp. He was stopped at the light when the driver of the smart car tried to squeeze by to his right but couldn't quite fit and had to stop with the truck to her left and an interstate retaining wall to her right. When the light turned green, the truck driver proceeded into his right turn not seeing the car stopped between him and the wall. It was, in fact, impossible for him to see the car through his right side-view mirror. Needless to say the smart car was crushed like an aluminum beer can against John Belushi's forehead. It was a pretty gruesome scene."

Just then, Drew stuck his head in the door and asked, "Sam, I need to discuss that 'Wrongful Death' case with you. When are you available?" He had been assigned to co-defend the case I had just described to Shmooky. I made brief introductions, but could not detect any judgment in Drew's reaction. He was clearly focused on the case, and when he is focused, he doesn't like to be distracted by things not relevant.

"I know you are busy Sam, but there is just one question I have right now: Did our truck have one of those signs on the back warning approaching drivers that it makes wide right turns?"

"I am not sure about that sign, but I do know that it had a sign that said: 'How is my driving? Call 1-800-EAT-SHIT,'" I quipped.

Drew looked at me with mild amusement, shook his head and walked off. I looked over at Shmooky and immediately felt embarrassed as I noticed the first hint of disapproval in her eyes. She looked puzzled as if she was thinking, is this guy for real? I immediately realized my last comment was in extremely poor taste given the gravity of the case. She didn't know me and couldn't possibly understand that I meant no disrespect to the dead girls. After twenty-seven years, this is how I cope.

I tried to explain, "Hey, I am just kidding. I use humor to keep my sanity in this business."

"Drew is the best lawyer in the office," I continued. "He is always supremely prepared, tough, no nonsense and gets great results without resorting to behaving like an animal. I am really happy he has been assigned to defend the case with me."

"Anyway, this isn't a law firm. We are corporate counsel for a large interstate trucking company, and I work solely for one client, my employer. I have worked for law firms before, but I prefer this type of practice. The hours are reasonable, and I have protection from the egomaniacal sociopaths who inhabit the upper-level partnership positions of most firms. I have worked in defense firms in which the partners stole my billable hours, took credit for my work and kept me insulated from the clients out of fear they might realize who was actually representing them. I worked seventy-hour weeks, including most Sundays. Yes, law firms are the last bastions of slavery in our flawed justice system. And it's not just the partners who will do anything to enrich themselves. It is also the associate attorneys who you think are your friends. Many of them will do just about anything to position themselves on the partnership track including brown-nosing and back-stabbing, to actually informing on their fellow associates. Trying to move up the partnership track in most law firms reminds me of when I smoked pot back in college: the more you suck, the higher you get."

"You smoke pot?" she asked with a giggle.

"Not since 1978, but I have fond memories of it. I did all of my deep thinking when I was stoned."

"So you haven't had a deep thought in thirty years?"

Boy, she was quick. This time I was the one who was left without a response, so I stuck out my tongue.

I loved the cute way she giggled so I continued with my rant. "So, if I am going to be stuck in this business for the next ten years, unfortunately, this is as good as it gets. Personally, I get much more satisfaction from tending bar. You certainly meet a more interesting class of people."

I could tell her amusement had changed to concern. She then said, "You sound so cynical."

"Well, maybe I am. Twenty-seven years is a long time to be doing something you were never crazy about to begin with. Since you are just starting out, my advice is to pick a career you are truly passionate about."

Still concerned, she asked, "Well, is there anything you are passionate about?"

"Me? Oh, not much anymore. I love golf and football, but could never dream of making a living at either. I am interested in sports betting, especially football. It is very challenging and you have to stay on your toes all week if you expect to make any money on the weekend. Maybe, instead of law school, after graduation, I should have gone out to Vegas with my college roommate. He is now the top picker in Nevada. Talk about passion: he has been doing it for more than thirty years but still gets up every morning foaming at the mouth. He makes an appearance on the show *VegasWorld* throughout the football season, and goes by the name of 'The Commissioner.'"

She was listening attentively, but I wanted to know more about her. "So what are you passionate about?" I asked.

"I have always wanted to work with children. Maybe special needs kids."

"You must have the patience of a saint," I said admiringly.

"But you raised a child."

"I am not sure I actually raised Alexa. It amazes me that she has turned out so well when you consider that both of her parents are lunatics. I adore her as I am sure your mother dearly loves you. So please, send her that e-mail."

She sent her mother a short e-mail assuring her she was safe and promising to send one periodically. When she was finished, she said, "I guess I better get going."

My heart sank. "I don't want you to go," I blurted without thinking of how it sounded.

"Well, I'm really not going anywhere. I'm around Wall Street pretty much every day. So I'll see you again, won't I?"

"Absolutely," I replied.

I took her down in the elevator to the lobby of the building. She thanked me for a wonderful day and like an idiot I awkwardly extended my hand as if to shake hers. She gave it a puzzled look before moving close to embrace me. I gave her a weak hug and kissed her on the top of her head, right on Chief Wahoo's grinning lips. We embraced for a couple moments before she smiled and said, "Good bye, Shmooky," before walking quickly away. She glanced back and smiled as she exited. That was our five-hour first date.

I kept watching her until she passed around the corner and was reminded of the scene in *The Godfather* in which Michael Corleone is in Sicily after killing the police captain, McCluskey. While in hiding, he is hit by the "thunderbolt." I'm referring to the girl he marries and who then gets blown up with a car bomb.

So this is what it feels like, I thought. In fifty-two years, I have never felt the thunderbolt until now. The feeling is difficult to describe as it is all-encompassing. From that point forward, not a moment would pass without her in my thoughts. She has the power to overwhelm me and doesn't even know it. All I can think about is our next meeting. When it hits, the aftershock of the thunderbolt isn't voluntary. It is more like a chemical reaction of some sort. It is also unconditional in that it's not based on her feeling the same way about me in return.

When I got back up to the office, I thought I could get a few hours of work done, but just as I sat down at my desk, Janeka, my long-time secretary stuck her head in the door. Janeka is my own personal Oprah. I could tell her anything, and she always seemed to have good advice on the serious subjects. However, she had little patience with me when I was feeling sorry for myself and had a biting sense of humor when my behavior was deserving of an insult.

"Sam, can I speak openly without you getting mad?"

"My ears are ringing, but when do I ever get mad? I know what you are going to say, and all I can say in response is that I would think that if people around here had enough work to do, they wouldn't have the time to keep their mind in the toilet."

"Stop rationalizing Sam. Who is that child?"

"She isn't a child; she is twenty and will be twenty-one in February."

"Twenty!? You have hemorrhoids older than that! Sam, I have been your assistant for fifteen years, and I'm worried. I know all about your divorce judgment last week, but this isn't the answer. You are fifty-two years old, and that girl is younger than your daughter."

"Janeka, please, trust me. It's not what you are thinking."

At that point, the phone buzzed, and I picked it up to tell the receptionist that I was not in.

"Janeka, you know what I hate most about practicing law?"

"Of course I do; you only tell me four or five times a day. But stop trying to change the subject."

"I do?"

"Yes. You are always telling me how much you hate answering discovery."

"Okay, I guess I do say that from time to time. Discovery takes away what little excitement there is in this job. Why should they be able to find out everything about my case?"

"Probably because *we* are able to find out everything about *their* case. So it's fair," she responded impatiently.

"But what if I don't want to know everything about their case in advance."

Janeka laughed as I said, "Wouldn't it be just as fair if both sides didn't know jack shit. Think of all the time it would save and how much more exciting and dramatic jury trials would be. Anyway, we are getting away from the point."

"There is a point here?" Janeka responded sarcastically.

"Yes, what I hate most, I mean second most, is talking to assholes on the phone. So from now on, I don't want any calls."

Now getting exasperated, she replied, "So, tell the receptionist."

"But I don't like talking to her. I find her very judgmental."

"Really? Lori?"

"You call her Lori; I call her 'The House Plant.' Anyway, the only time I ever say anything to her is to tell her that I'm not here."

"So?"

"So she knows I am here because when I don't pick up the phone, it is always because I'm really not here, but when I do pick up, it is only when I am here and telling her that I'm not here. But she knows I am here, and when I see her as I am walking to the men's room, she gives me a look like I am a frigging liar."

"I see. Have you been drinking already today?"

"I will ignore that shot. So the only solution is for her to tell everyone I am not here."

"Every time?"

"Yes."

"Even when she knows you are here?"

"Especially then. Look, Janeka, I know you think I am odd."

"Odd? I don't think that at all. I think you are one of those crazy white boys my momma warned me about."

"Please, I am begging you, just for a moment, stop messing with me. I have carefully thought all of this out, and I don't want to repeat it. Frankly, I am not sure I am capable."

"Sorry."

"No problem. So yes, I want you to tell her that I'm always not here."

"But what if it is an important call?"

"Then have her put the call through to voicemail. I will periodically check it, and then I will decide whether I am here or not."

"Gotcha," she replied dismissively.

"Great."

Janeka left my office and started packing up to leave. "Where are you going?" I asked. "We have a lot of work to catch-up on."

"No. *You* have a lot of work to catch up on. It's 4:30, and I am leaving."

"It is?"

"Yeah, you have been fooling around with that child all afternoon and lost track of time. I have church choir practice tonight, and I'm going to pray for Jesus to help you, because I think you need it. I think you're losing your mind."

"Janeka, I appreciate your prayers, but that isn't necessary. I am good."

"I am sure you are good," she replied. "But are you all right? There is a difference you know."

5. Brown-eyed Girl

So hard to find my way
Now that I'm all on my own
I saw you just the other day
My, how you have grown
                    —Van Morrison

I met Shmooky for lunch every day for the next three weeks. I arranged my schedule so that I would not miss a single day. The feeling that it was all too good to be true overwhelmed my thoughts. I would anxiously wait all morning for the stroke of 11:30, trying desperately to concentrate on my work. There was always the fear that she would not be there when I arrived, so I walked with childish anticipation to our usual spot at the Cantina. We sat at the same outside table every day, and there was always a huge sense of relief when I saw her waiting for me. I felt like a love-sick schoolboy when our eyes met. She always greeted me with a warm smile, a "Hey, Shmooky" and a peck on the cheek. In those early days, I felt terribly vulnerable. My biggest fear at that time was saying or doing something that might offend her. I was worried that if I upset her, I would never see her again. It was only after she started asking me a lot of personal questions that I felt a little more comfortable inquiring about her life.

That day I asked, "So what do you want to do with your life?"

"I thought about working at Disney World. That is why I came here, but they don't pay very much."

"You are right about that. I guess they didn't get to be one of the world's most successful corporations by paying their employees above the minimum they can get away with."

"So I thought I would like to be an elementary school teacher. I love children."

"Do you want children of your own?" I asked.

"Of course I do. Some day, but there is so much I need to accomplish first."

"Like what?" I probed.

"Oh, lots of things," she said evasively.

"Try not to be so specific," I quipped. She laughed, but I was getting frustrated. Every time I tried to get her to open up to me about her dreams and desires, she would always abruptly change the subject. She was hiding something from me, but I couldn't put my finger on it. The more I tried to probe, the more she focused her questions on me. She was especially interested in lawyers and all of the dirty secrets of our profession. This only encouraged me to rant on and on. I thought I was boring her, but the more I told her, the more she wanted to know.

"Do you like being a lawyer?" she asked curiously.

"Oh, during the first few years even a skeptic like me had a little bit of idealism and felt I was making a positive contribution to society. I haven't felt that way in a long, long time. There may be uglier ways of making a living but there are few less honest. Maybe I have been at it too long. After twenty-seven years, I must admit that I am pretty burned-out. That is why I started bartending. I want to have fun and meet a diverse group of people. Don't get me wrong, there are some great people in my profession, but it seems that with each passing year, there are fewer and fewer of them. Unfortunately, there is much truth to the stereotype. I am sure every profession has a few members who bring shame to the rest, but we seem to attract much more than our share of greedy, self-righteous, mean-spirited egomaniacs."

"The one thing that is definitely more advanced here than in Ohio are the personal injury lawyer TV commercials. Some of them are so tacky. Do you know those guys?"

"Sure, this is still a small town. I know all of them. I felt that way earlier in my career, but now I really see nothing wrong with it. It's a First Amendment issue. They have a right to advertise just like any other business."

"But some of them are on TV and radio day and night," she said with revulsion.

"They are performing a service, just like a plumber or electrician. Why shouldn't they advertise? Anyway, the ads aren't the issue; it's the BS that goes with it that pisses me off. Why can't they just admit they are in a business and stop trying to convince us that they are saving the world? Many of them are self-righteous turds who claim to be fighting for truth and justice but, of course, never mention that their cut of justice is a cool 40 percent. Imagine the shock people go through when they settle their lawsuit and once costs are deducted their lawyer walks away with more than they get. In some complex and time consuming cases, the lawyer actually earns a good portion of his fee, but in most cases, their compensation is staggering if it were measured hourly."

"Is there anything that can be done?" she asked inquisitively.

"Regulation might help, but these guys will fight tooth and nail any attempt to reform their industry. Believe me, any business in which a pretty-boy, intellectual mediocrity like John Edwards can become a millionaire forty times over is in desperate need of regulation. Their hypocrisy is boundless. The trial lawyers give tens of millions of dollars to the Democratic Party. This is the same party that wants government regulation of the medical profession, the insurance industry, what we eat, what we drive, where we can send our kids to school, and what, if any, guns we can own, just to name a few. But the mere mention of Tort Reform has them howling at the moon. They will settle for nothing less than unrestricted, unfettered, robber-baron capitalism."

"The worst was a guy I worked for very early in my career. I should actually thank him for squelching with gallons of putrid water the last flaming embers of my idealism."

"How poetic," she laughed.

"You like that? I have a million of them. Anyway, he took me to lunch as part of my job interview and told me that he never plans to retire because he is passionate about his work. I was young, and at the time, I thought it was commendable to be that much in love with the law. But after working for him for a while, I realized the real reason he doesn't want to retire. He is obsessed with the power he has over people. He loved the daily battle with other attorneys as long as the playing field was tilted in his favor and the case was a slam-dunk. He had mastered the lethal combination of winning at all costs while criticizing with righteous indignation any opponent who was as adept at it as he was. But most of all, he loved terrorizing people who couldn't fight back: his employees. He was a miser but worse than that, he got off on manipulating their lives by keeping them in a constant state of job insecurity. If he were the head of a country instead of a law firm, he would put Joe Stalin to shame. I gave up five years of my life for that asshole and finally quit, totally disillusioned. He couldn't hide his anger when I left—not because I was leaving, but because I left on my own terms. He hated that."

"Does it matter which side you are on?"

"I have been doing this much too long to believe either side has a monopoly on virtue. In a typical personal injury trial, each lawyer goes into court and pulls out his dick. They then piss on each other. Whoever emerges smelling the best wins, and it is usually a pretty close call."

"What if you don't have a dick?" she laughed.

"You really don't need one. The women in this business are usually meaner—much meaner than the men. Hands down."

"But overall, you must believe your side is more virtuous. Don't you?"

"I used to think so, but over the years, I have learned that we have more than our fair share of villains on the defense side. There is a lot of frustration since, although more often than not, the defense lawyer is every bit the equal in skill, knowledge and experience, few of us make anything close to what even a mediocre plaintiff's attorney can make. This pent-up frustration can cause depression and in the extreme case, rage."

"Rage?"

"Oh yeah, the enraged defense lawyer. These are the bullies in my business. Whatever their underlying issues may be, their rage is manifested in self-righteous arrogance and intimidation. They are always right, never accept responsibility for their mistakes, and when challenged, will resort to the most unprofessional behavior from dropping F-bombs to subtle physical intimidation. They are hated by opposing attorneys and co-workers alike. But it is the hapless support staff, who have no power to resist, who are victimized the most. Like all bullies, this type of lawyer smells weakness and reserves his or her worst behavior for those who can't fight back. This will usually go unchecked indefinitely, because even those who have the power to take them on usually conclude that to do so would be so unpleasant, it just isn't worth it."

"I have worked with many of these people over the years, and sometimes I think the Bar should require anger management therapy after the first offense. At least my company has mandatory civility guidelines, a first in this business. I have to give them credit for that. We are supposed to be professional lawyers, not wrestlers. I often wondered whether there is a strategy behind this uncivil behavior. Several years ago, I asked one of the worst examples of this type why he chooses to live in a constant state of rage and why it didn't seem to bother him to be the most despised man in the courthouse. He told me that he wants to make the litigation experience so unpleasant for the plaintiff and his attorney that they will be anxious to settle quickly and at less than fair value. I thought about it for a moment and immediately concluded that this strategy is not only idiotic but counterproductive. It conflicts with everything I have learned about human nature. If you treat people like garbage, you are more likely to force them to resist your bullying, which only prolongs the litigation, thereby increasing the cost to your client. My father was a tax lawyer, not a litigator. He never had to deal with tactics I am forced to confront day in and day out. However, he was familiar with what I would be up against, and when I started practicing, he sent me a copy of the novel, *To Kill a Mockingbird.* Although that story involved a criminal case, the principles are the same. Atticus Finch treated people with dignity and respect. He never raised his voice or lost his cool and was always the consummate professional. My father told me to try to model my professional behavior after him. I have tried to do so, but it hasn't been easy, and maintaining this ideal only adds to my stress level. After twenty-seven years, I have had enough, but what choice do I have?"

Shmooky responded, "You always have choices."

"Wait a second. I am not quite finished," I laughed.

"There is more?"

"Of course, unfortunately."

"The other life form is also seen frequently in the non-legal world. These are the ubiquitous, back-stabbing brown-nosers. Rather than succeeding or failing on their own merits, they feel the need to work behind the scenes collecting tidbits of information to present to the boss in an effort to discredit those they are in competition with for money and advancement. I have known at least one of these lawyers in every firm I have worked for over the years. The thing that puzzles me the most is that virtually all of them have been pretty good lawyers and would likely have succeeded without selling their soul. There was one guy who always tried to pump me for my feelings about office policy, management, etc. while pretending he was in agreement. Then, when I would go in for my performance review, somehow, management was aware of feelings I had expressed to only one other person. I wonder who told them!"

Shmooky laughed. "Sounds like the office can be a nightmare."

"It certainly can be. I survive by trying to ignore it. That is why I think that if you really want to teach in elementary school, you should go for it; if you can teach special needs kids, all the better. Do something that will have a positive impact on the world."

"Unfortunately, Sam, you were right when you took that shot at me that first day in the restaurant. I dropped out of high school mid-way through my senior year. I was too screwed up at the time to realize the consequences."

"That isn't the end of the world. Let's work on getting you a GED and then we can start discussing what to do next."

"You want to help me?"

"Of course."

I was hoping to get a commitment from her but again, she backed away politely. She smiled appreciatively but then said, "I will think about it, but now I am concerned about you. It doesn't sound like you are very happy at work."

"I'm not, but it almost pays the bills."

"Has it ever gotten to the point that you were so frustrated you felt like just saying, 'That's it; I am done'?"

"Oh, all the time."

"Then why don't you?"

"Well, when Alexa graduates from college in the spring, I just might do that. Actually, I worked with a lawyer a few years ago who did extensive research on how to disappear without a trace."

"You mean kill yourself? Please don't do that."

"No, of course not. I would never consider that no matter how bad things get. I am referring to the idea of just disappearing without a trace. No ex-wives, no IRS, no creditors, etc. knowing where to find you."

Shmooky listened with rapt attention. "That really sounds interesting."

"Yes," I replied. "But this same guy also did extensive research and concluded that it was healthier to elevate your feet when taking a shit."

"What!?" she giggled.

"I am serious. Every time I saw him walking to the men's room carrying a couple of phone books, I knew what he was up to. I started to question all of his theories after that."

Shmooky's face was now red from giggling uncontrollably. "You have the cutest laugh," I said. I was again having one of those thunderbolt moments. I just wanted to hold her tight in my arms. She didn't realize that I was off in a daydream when she asked, "Whatever happened to him?"

I was so lost in looking at her that I said, "Who?"

"The guy you were just talking about, dummy. The guy with the phone books."

"Oh," I said, returning to reality. "He didn't disappear. I see him around from time to time, but he still doesn't give a shit. I guess the phone books didn't work."

I parted with her that day feeling great, but still concerned. In addition to lunch she called me several times a day and every night. We would chat for hours about every subject imaginable, and I was always amazed at the level of her knowledge despite her lack of formal education. However, every time I tried to return the conversation to her life, she pulled away. After several weeks, I still had no idea how she spent the rest of her time, where she worked or where she lived. She always seemed happy to see me, but I detected she was in pain and crying out for help. Maybe she was afraid she would scare me off if I knew these answers. Part of me wanted to force the issue, but I was still concerned that if I upset her, she would disappear. I had fallen for her hard, and the thought of her leaving was unbearable to me.

6. Words of Love

Hold me close and tell me how you feel
Tell me love is real
—Buddy Holly

When we met for lunch the next day, I was hoping we could get off the legal topics and focus on her. We decided to try a new place, and I picked Jesse's Bistro since I worked there as a bartender a couple of nights a week and knew the food was good. I also wanted people I know to get used to the idea of seeing her with me. Sure, they would be shocked at first, but they were going to have to get over it. Shmooky was my girlfriend as far as I was concerned, and no amount of disapproval was going to change my mind. It was jealousy anyway. From the guys, it had to do with the fact that they long ago lost in their own marriages the kind of passion I had for her. As for the women, they couldn't help but think back to the day when they possessed her innocent, untarnished beauty.

She was waiting outside when I arrived and greeted me with a big kiss, this time on the lips. She was in a playful mood which only heightened my desire to be near her.

"This is a nice place. Should I take off my hat?" she asked with a look of concern.

"That is up to you. Personally, I think Chief Wahoo is appropriate for every level of dining."

She laughed as she took it off, revealing her teenybopper ponytail. The manager, Steve, opened the door and greeted me, "The Old Dude. What's up?" I introduced her as my friend, Sammie. He sat us down and winked at me with a somehow knowing look.

"Why did he just call you 'The Old Dude'? Why not just call you dude?"

"Because there is only one Dude and that is Jeff Bridges, who is, in my opinion, the most under-rated actor in Hollywood. I am The Old Dude because I am, I guess, obsessed with the movie, *The Big Lebowski*."

"I must've missed that one."

"You're kidding. It may be the greatest movie of all time."

"Don't you think that is just a little bit of an exaggeration?"

"Not at all. It is definitely in the top five and had the movie involved golf instead of bowling it would have been the best of all time without question."

"Sam, like, I am a big movie buff, and I have barely heard of it, have no desire to see it and you are comparing it to like, *Gone with the Wind*."

"First of all, if you have never seen *The Big Lebowski* and want to consider yourself a movie aficionado, you have a gigantic hole in your resume. Actually, Shmooky, *The Big Lebowski* is far superior to *Gone with the Wind*."

She gasped.

"Yes, that story only deals with lives destroyed during and after the Civil War. Jeff Lebowski, or The Dude, is a brilliant composite of a pothead, alcoholic, Christian and Eastern philosopher who finds himself victimized by a series of highly complex events not of his own making. The story is developed brilliantly with a convoluted plotline ending with The Dude resolving each crisis. Despite being continuously drunk and stoned, he ultimately prevails over the forces of evil. Margaret Mitchell could never write such a story."

"You are totally brain-damaged, dude," she said, now laughing hysterically. "The five greatest movies of all time are: *Gone with the Wind, Sabrina, My Fair Lady, Breakfast at Tiffany's* and *Casablanca.*"

I sat there in silence for what had to be two or three minutes before she continued to provoke me. "You are left speechless by the infallibility of my selections."

"I think you over-estimate yourself," I replied.

"Oh please, tell me more," she said as she challenged and mocked me.

"Tell you more. Okay, I must confess my silence just now had more to do with my surprise at your choices. Those are some very old films. I would have thought you would have picked some of the movies Alexa used to watch over and over: *The Breakfast Club, Pretty in Pink, Ferris Bueller's Day Off,* and *Sixteen Candles;* that sort of thing."

"I love those movies, too, but the question is: what are the five best movies of all time? Now please, tell me why I am wrong. I could use a good laugh."

I actually loved it when she teased me. She is completely unimpressed with age and experience and feels she can stand toe-to-toe with me on virtually any subject. That day it was movies, but she can also present solid positions on subjects ranging from politics, the war on terror and global warming to sports, interpersonal relationships to the latest asshole to appear on *American Idol.* She blew me away with her movie picks. Every time I conclude that I have defined her, she destroys the very foundation of my beliefs. I gaze into her eyes and see a woman-child who looks back at me admiringly as she reconstructs my shattered psyche. But she is so much more than that. It is now an inescapable fact and pointless to try to suppress it that it is I who admire her.

I did not know what she did when I wasn't around, but it was clear to me that she had the intellect to do anything she wanted. Debating her was such a refreshing change from Jen who would have a hissy-fit if you disagreed with her. It always ended with her calling me an idiot or a drunk before she announced she was going shopping.

Since she was in a feisty mood, I deliberately picked five movies to bring out the most explosive reaction. Not that they are not my favorites. They are, but I avoided any potentially diplomatic selections. "Listen to me carefully, and you will learn something about cinema. The five best movies of all time are: *The Godfather, The Godfather II, Goodfellas, Scarface* and *The Big Lebowski,* with an honorable mention for *Caddyshack.* This is not subject to debate."

Shmooky gave me a Bronx cheer as she continued to laugh uncontrollably. "You are such a nut. But a cute nut."

"No one has called me cute in about twenty-five years."

"It has nothing to do with physical appearance."

"Gee, thanks."

"It is the way you seem to glide through the world semi-serious, but apparently, it somehow works for you."

"I am always serious. What do you mean?"

"I mean the 1950s era reading glasses always hanging precariously from the tip of your nose, the bathrobe, the bedroom slippers with black socks, a Scotch in your hand at all times, the sports betting line, the awful golf art, the Dean Martin music and the stench cigars. Should I go on? That's a lot of weird shit, dude. But then you get up every morning and somehow put yourself back together to return to your other life as a functioning professional. It's almost like you are two separate people. I just find it very amusing. Cute."

"Hey, it works for me," I said as I thought, *Geez, she picked up a lot during the surprise visit she made to my condo a couple of nights ago.* I live in one of those new "smart" buildings, which has a security system more elaborate than Guantanamo's. You have to have a special square key to activate the key pad, which then requires your fingerprint to be scanned before the door clicks open. This is all done under the watchful eyes of the concierge to prevent intruders from tail-gating in behind a resident. The process is then repeated in the elevator, and you can only get off at your own floor. The system was designed to prevent assholes from showing up, unannounced, at your door. I had lived there since separating from Jen, and this was the first time I received an unexpected knock. It took real ingenuity to get past security. I was impressed but also completely unprepared. She took one look at me and started laughing hysterically. I said, "What?" two or three times, even though I knew what was funny. She was careful not to risk hurting my feelings and kept replying, "Nothing, nothing."

"How did you get up here?" I asked in amazement.

"It was easy, although I did have to ride the elevator for 45 minutes waiting for someone to stop on your floor." She was immediately drawn to the windows as the entire east side of the condo faced the lake. She said, "Wow, what a view," and then started to closely examine my bookcases. "I love these old black and white photos. Who are these people?"

"Dead Goombas," I replied.

She gave me a look of disapproval, and I said, "What?"

"Nothing. I am just a little sensitive about that sort of thing. When I was in high school the rich girls called me 'The little Pollack.'"

"That's mean," I replied. "I would have called you 'the cute little Pollack.'"

She rolled her eyes and said, "So what are you doing?"

"Just listening to Dean Martin and reviewing some of my notes on that death case."

"You are worried about that case, aren't you?" she said as she moved closer to view the computer screen.

"I suppose."

"Yuck!" she recoiled in an almost juvenile manner.

"What?" I asked in panic.

"Jesus Christo!" she replied in Spanish. "That cigar estinks."

"It is not even lit," I protested.

Upon seeing from the look on her face that she was in no way less repulsed, I moved away leaving her at the computer. I knew she was kidding, but after years of slow, grueling mental abuse my self-esteem was so fragile, I placed the cigar in an ash tray and darted from the room beating a disorderly retreat to tend to the open wound. I went into the bathroom and gargled a half bottle of Scope before changing into jeans and a T-shirt.

When I got back she was busy reading my file.

"You need to settle this case. This is such a sad story," she said, shaking her head with a heartsick look. "They were so young. Their parents must be devastated."

"I am sure they are," I replied. "But the truth is liability is very questionable. This is the type of case that all defense lawyers dread. It wasn't the truck driver's fault, but there are two dead teenagers. They were both beautiful, both A students, and both popular. What am I supposed to do? I have to walk a tightrope with the jury. If I slam the kid who was driving on her stupidity too hard, they will crucify me. Settlement of the case has to be the company's decision. If I let on in any way that I am apprehensive, they will think I don't have the guts to take it to trial."

"That's stupid," she replied in an exasperated tone.

"Maybe, but that is how the game is played. Now you know why I hate my job. Most of my cases are jokes, but this one keeps me awake at night, and I have enough trouble sleeping without this kind of stress."

Shmooky must have realized that my tension level was rising, because she left me at the computer. I assumed that she went to the bathroom, but she returned a couple of minutes later dressed in my bathrobe, black socks and slippers with my used cigar in her mouth. She walked up, took off my reading glasses, and put them on the end of her cute little nose before announcing: "This is my imitation of Sam." She had me down, including the arthritic limp I had to walk-off every time I rose from a chair. "Sam, you kinda remind me of Groucho Marx," she taunted.

I had a good laugh as I walked up to remove the cigar. "How could you put that soggy thing in your mouth?" I asked with amused disgust.

"I don't mind swapping spit with you, even if it is tinged Honduran. Having that taste in my mouth will cancel you out," she giggled.

Suddenly overwhelmed with passion, I took the cigar from her mouth and flung it across the room. Apparently, she noticed I was no longer smiling as she took a half step back and seemed slightly confused before I pulled her close to kiss her with a passion I never thought I could possibly possess. We were both breathless as we momentarily pushed slightly apart. I looked into her eyes cautiously, not knowing whether I would see polite revulsion or the desire I had hoped for.

"What are you doing, Sam?"

"A kiss to seal our fate," I replied.

She smiled as she moved her sweet, pink lips back into position and closed her eyes. I kissed her again, this time more deeply, before we parted awkwardly. Now I was the one who was confused and diverted my eyes, as if embarrassed by my lack of self control. I am sure she sensed that my hesitation was confirmation I could not do what was supposed to happen next.

"I guess I should go," she said as she pulled off the bathrobe and headed quickly for the exit.

"See you tomorrow?" I asked hopefully, as she opened the door.

"Of course," she replied.

As soon as the door closed, Dean Martin started singing "Ain't that a kick in the head," and I collapsed into the recliner kicking myself. Why didn't I ask her to stay? I wondered. The answer was clear. I had fallen for her hard and didn't want to risk screwing things up. I was seemingly willing to continue to fantasize my love rather than risk the slightest chance of offending her.

Returning my thoughts to the present I said, "You think you have me all figured out don't you."

"Not true, old dude. I think I would have to spend years with you to do that."

"Sounds good to me. That reminds me, you have never commented on the way we parted when you came up to visit the other night."

"No comment is required. It told me all I need to know."

"You seem very confident, but I am not sure what you are talking about."

She focused her eyes on mine as if she could look directly into my soul and said, "Men are very courageous when they don't really care about a woman. They will take their shot and if they fail, nothing is lost. But even the most mature and polished man will approach the woman he loves and behave like a clumsy schoolboy if he is uncertain of her feelings. It was that bashful look on your face after you finally kissed me that gave you away. You won't admit, at least not yet, how you feel about me. But I can tell."

I had no response, and I am sure I looked guilty as charged as our lunch was suddenly interrupted by the sound of a screeching female voice from across the crowded restaurant. "Sam! Sam, how have you been?"

"Just great, Christy."

"This must be your beautiful daughter, Alexa."

"Actually, no; this is Sammie Wilenski, a friend of mine."

"After a few awkward moments of stunned silence I asked, "Are you all right Christy?" She then finally snapped out of it and said, "Of course. Listen Sam, I have to run but give me a call and we will do lunch next week."

"Sure," I responded. "I will look forward to it."

As Christy moved out of ear-shot, Shmooky looked at me as only she can and said, "Do lunch? What is that, a term of art used by today's asshole petit bourgeois?"

"My, haven't we become judgmental?"

"You are not really going to 'do lunch' with that awful woman, are you?"

"You didn't like her?"

"How could I like her? She looked at me as if I had a twelve-inch dildo sticking out of my pie-hole." She briefly paused and then said, "Well? Why are you laughing at me?"

"I was just picturing you with that dildo." I laughed before responding earnestly. "Look Shmooky, she's just jealous. She recently turned forty, needs to shed a few pounds and has to glue on her face every morning. You are so adorable. I just want to squeeze you and never let go. I would never get tired of looking at you. I am sure she started watching us as soon as she saw you and could see just how obvious it is that you have me completely spellbound. She knew you are not my daughter."

At that moment, her entire demeanor changed as the supremely self-confident and formidable Ms. Wilenski transformed herself instantaneously into Shmooky. She reached across the table, took my hand and gently kissed it while keeping her eyes focused on mine. My heart pounded as I searched for any possible clue that would force me to accept the inevitable truth that this was all just a game to her. I found nothing other than sincerity and then vulnerability as a light mist clouded her doe-like eyes. Moments like this compelled me to reassess the conclusion I had reached long ago: that I never have and never will experience mutual romantic love.

7. Everything I Own

I would give anything I own
Give up my life, my heart, my home
I would give everything I own
Just to have you back again
Just to touch you once again
                    —David Gates and Bread

As fast as it started, it was over. I completely lost touch with her after that lunch at Jesse's Bistro, and I was frantic. She knew how to find me, but I had no idea how to contact her. All I had was a cell phone number that was now disconnected. Did she move back to Ohio? If so, why wouldn't she tell me? Why didn't she at least call to say goodbye? Every day, I would spend my lunch hour walking around central downtown. On the Friday of the second week without contact, I even asked some of the young Goths, metal-heads, tattooed assholes and other assorted losers if they had seen her. I walked up to the one I thought was most approachable and said, "I am looking for a young woman." He responded dismissively, "We all are, dude," and turned away. Maybe they could detect my revulsion, but the others who would talk to me gave me only an abrupt "No" without offering any ideas or help.

Al made his usual 10:00 a.m. call the following day to discuss the weekend's match-ups. I was in such a moribund state, I didn't even know who was playing and really didn't care.

"Al, I lost her," I said dejectedly. "It has been two full weeks now. She is gone."

"How old did you say she was?"

"I didn't, but if you must know, she is twenty."

"Oh, she is VYP. Very young . . ."

"That's enough!" I interrupted. "We haven't even come close to having sex. Not that it is any of your damn business."

"No sex yet, and you are this whacked-out?"

"You are going to think this is crazy," I said earnestly, "but I think I am in love with her."

"You are one *meshugge goyim*" (crazy gentile).

"That may be, but I am going to have to take a pass on this weekend. My head isn't into it."

"All right, call me if you change your mind," he said in disappointment before hanging up. He was annoyed, but I couldn't help it. I spent the rest of the weekend alone, drinking heavily. I had the games on but couldn't tell you who was playing, who won or, more importantly, who covered.

Maybe Al is right. Maybe I am *meshugge*. I couldn't get that stupid word, "shmooky," out of my head. The word is unintelligible and beneath comical. It is silly. Too silly to call a puppy much less your own child, but yet I found saying it almost intoxicating even without the aid of a few Scotches. Had her father invented it? Thinking no one else could possibly have uttered such nonsense, I Googled it and was shocked to get 1,730 hits. It is actually defined in *Mo' Urban Dictionary*. The word was apparently invented by Sir Bwain Johnson. "Shmooky: Most likely a 'shmooky' will be a random person who has no purpose and authority in our daily lives whatsoever." *An absolutely accurate definition*, I thought, *if it is applied to my reaction to her the day we first met at the restaurant, but there must be more*. I scanned the page and found the word "shmook," a word invented by

Eskibear, and defined as, "someone who is very cute." That certainly applies, but here it is, a word invented by Yasmin. "Shmook-ee-poo: a lover who is far beyond your every imaginable reach."

I left for work in a fog on Monday morning, and after three more unproductive days and sleepless nights, I called George, an old friend and golf buddy whose brother-in-law is an Orlando motorcycle cop. I asked him to lunch downtown and to bring Larry the cop with him. I also asked him not to mention anything to his wife, Andrea, who was Jen's best friend. George and Andrea were our only mutual friends who tried to stay neutral during the long and acrimonious divorce litigation, but the strain had taken its toll on them.

The next day, I took a table outside at the Lakeside Cafe. It was a beautiful autumn day, and the place was packed. George was also a big fan of *The Big Lebowski,* and every time we met, we would start off with some dialog. We were set to play golf on Saturday morning, so when George walked up to my table he said: *"Let me tell ju somesing bendeho: ju try any of that crazy chit, pulling jor piece out on the golf course, and I am going to take it away, stick it up jor ass and pull the trigger until it goes click."*

I responded with my favorite line in the whole movie: *"Well, like, that's your opinion man."*

I then got serious and asked, "Where is Larry?"

"Oh, as usual, he is running a little late."

Just then I heard the sound of a motorcycle approaching on Central Boulevard. It was him, and when he parked, got off his bike, and walked up the steps to the restaurant, everyone stopped eating, stopped talking, and stared as he entered the patio. He was an imposing figure at 6 feet 5 inches, 280 pounds with huge muscles covering every inch. In his uniform and helmet, he looked like a Terminator. When he arrived at the table, we shook hands and sat down. I told him, "You know, I wish I could enter a restaurant like that."

"Like what?"

"Like, fuck all of you and if you don't like it, do something about it."

He laughed, but the first thing he noticed were my football betting notes that I had been reviewing prior to George's arrival.

"You know that shit's illegal," he said.

"Yeah right," I replied with a laugh. "What do you want this weekend?"

"I was thinking of taking Maryland, Kansas, and Notre Dame in a three-way," Larry replied.

I thought about it for a moment and then burst out laughing.

"What's wrong?" Larry demanded. "Is that a bad bet?"

"No, I was just imagining Ralph Freidgen, Mark Mangino and Charlie Weiss (the coaches at each school who all weighed well over 300 pounds apiece) in a three-way."

"Damn, that's gross man. You are sick to even think of shit like that. Anyway, put me down for a hunge."

"Got it," I replied.

We had lunch and talked about Larry's sex life, always an amusing topic of discussion. Finally he asked me, "When are you going to come out to The Cosmopolitan with us?"

"Am I supposed to bring a date to these soirées?" I asked.

"Are you fucking kidding me? Why take sand when you are going to the beach. You are divorced now. I can guarantee you that you will hook up with a hot, young one."

I then raised the issue I had wanted him to check for me. "Listen, Larry, speaking of that, I need your help."

"Whatever I can do, counselor," he assured.

"Several weeks ago, I met this girl down on Wall Street. I used to see her every day, and we got to be good friends, at least so I thought. Anyway, I haven't seen her in almost three weeks, and she has made no attempt to contact me. I am really worried that something has happened to her."

George then interrupted, "What do you mean by a girl? Is she a friend or a . . .?"

"A what?" I asked, now irritated.

Larry asked, "How old is she?"

George was taking a drink from his water glass just as I answered "twenty." At that moment, Larry punched me in my left shoulder while shouting "You Dog!" My whole body moved to the right from the playful blow as George, upon hearing my answer, spit up his water all over my right sleeve.

"Jesus Christ, George! Say it, don't spray it."

"Twenty!?" George gasped, still choking from the water. "She is younger than Alexa. Have you lost what's left of your mind?"

"George, if you tell Andrea about this I am going to bust a cap in your ass," I threatened, only half joking. "She will tell Jen and then Jen will accuse me of being *Lolita's* Humbert Humbert. I don't want to hear any of that garbage."

"What does she do?" Larry asked.

"How the hell should I know? I haven't asked to review her frigging W-2."

"Jeez Sam, calm down dude; I am here to help."

"Sorry, Larry. I am losing it. I haven't been able to sleep in days."

Larry then pulled out his pad and asked, "What is her name?"

"Sammie."

George, still shaking his head said, "You are killing me, Sam."

"What does she look like?" Larry continued.

"Uh, she is about five foot one or two at the most, and maybe a hundred pounds, brown hair, brown eyes and very, very, very cute. You got that?"

"Yeah, three very's," Larry laughed as George continued to shake his head in disbelief.

"How does she typically dress?" Larry continued.

"Pretty much the same every day. Blue jeans, faded with one or two holes. A T-shirt, usually red, green or blue. White, very worn sneakers. Oh, and this should help. She uses a Cleveland Browns backpack as a purse and always wears a Cleveland Indians baseball cap—the one with the Chief Wahoo logo head."

George then interrupted and said, "You know, Sam, native Americans find Chief Wahoo very offensive."

"Well, they are crazy." I then added, using a faux Indian accent, "Chief Wahoo, him great warrior and great leader of his tribe."

Larry laughed and George said as he was getting up from the table, "You are such an A-hole. I will see you Saturday morning at Dubsdread. Our tee-time is 8:05 a.m."

"Yeah, and I am bringing my piece," I said as we parted.

My friendship with George had taken an interesting turn since our last golf trip to Southern Pines, North Carolina in mid-summer. The trip provided us with a couple of golf stories for the ages, but I also managed to injure him, although I deny it was my fault. We went up for a three-day weekend and golf on Friday and Saturday was completely uneventful.

Home of the world famous Pinehurst courses, Southern Pines is noted for its unlimited choices of golf courses and where there are golf courses there are titty bars. I had four or five Scotches with dinner that Saturday evening, so I was already lit when we arrived at the Booby Trap. We sat at the main stage and enjoyed hours of exotic dancing, Scotch and cigars.

I always loved the term "exotic." When I think of an exotic dance, I think of *Salome's Dance of the Seven Veils.* You know, the dance King Herrod loved so much it cost John the Baptist his head. Dancing nude is not exotic. It may be entertaining, but it is not exotic unless the dancer has mastered the art. It starts with the costume. For once, I would like to see someone come out dressed as an old-fashioned secretary, complete with a white dress-shirt, black string tie, black rimmed glasses and hair tied up in a bun. Or what about dressed as a cop, nurse, meter maid, or soldier? I am sick of the fucking whore outfits. Stimulate my imagination, bee-otch. It would also help if they took dancing lessons. Most of them can't dance and have no idea what to do with the pole. It is not there to hold up the ceiling! I get emotional about this shit.

Most strippers will tell you that they are really nice girls or they are in medical school or have three or four kids at home to support and receive nothing from the dead-beat dad(s). I will believe anything from a chick with a nice rack, and I want to give them a decent tip, but I need to be entertained. Bimbos in whore costumes that can't dance don't do it for me. But I put up with it and did so that night.

On Sunday morning, I woke up with an awesome hang-over. I had no recollection of how we got back to the hotel. I assume George drove, at least I hope so. I tried to take two or three ibuprofen but George warned me that taking ibuprofen for a hang-over can cause severe liver damage.

"You will be better off taking six aspirin," he warned.

"Oh, that makes a lot of sense," I replied. "So if I cut my hand playing golf, my blood will be so thin I will bleed to death, but at least my liver will be in good shape."

George replied with more than a trace of irritation. "Look, I don't know why I am concerned about you. You snored like a mother-fucker all night long, and I haven't had a wink of sleep."

"Yeah, I snore deliberately to give me an edge on the course, you A-hole."

I wondered how the FDA arrived at that conclusion. I could see them doing an exhaustive case study using fifty alcoholics suffering from hang-over headaches. After a few years of observation, they start to die off. The autopsies reveal extensive liver damage. Of course, it must have been caused by the fucking ibuprofen!

I took six aspirin and headed to breakfast. It was an impressive smorgasbord. Scrambled eggs, home fries, and sausage links washed down by four or five cups of coffee that must have been laced with Red Bull. I was cured by the time we reached the course. George had beaten me on Friday, but I came back on Saturday. This was for all the honor and glory and with a $2 Nassau, I teed off determined to kick his pseudo-intellectual ass.

As Basil Rathbone would say, the game was afoot. I rushed out to a quick lead taking two of the first three holes. Then it started. I could feel the gurgling in my stomach extending into my intestines. The pressure started building like Mt. St. Helens. By the time we completed the seventh hole, I had to take a wicked shit. *No problem,* I thought. Two more holes and we would be back at the clubhouse. I still held a two-hole lead so there was no reason to panic. I slowly released gas as we played to keep the pressure bearable. I have heard it said that everyone loves their own brand, but if these farts could have been bottled, a terrorist could have used it as a weapon of mass destruction.

As we reached the ninth tee, disaster struck. "Where is the fucking clubhouse?" I barked.

"How the hell should I know?" George replied.

I ran back to the cart and looked at the map on the scorecard. "This can't be."

"What can't be?"

"This is one of those courses that don't return to the clubhouse at the turn. We are out in the middle of fucking nowhere."

"So what?"

"So, I have to burn a mule. You know; take a shit, that's what."

George laughed, but I failed to see the humor. I was prairie-dogging, and there was no way I could compete in this condition. He then tried to act as if he was concerned, but I knew he was faking. He smelled blood—or was it my farts? This was his chance to win, and he was enjoying seeing me suffer.

George took the tenth and the eleventh hole. The score was now tied, with me sweating and straining to keep my sphincter shut. The match was over unless I could find someplace to evacuate. This was a links course, and there were no woods. I was so desperate that I was grasping at any possible solution. George took the twelfth hole, but on the thirteenth fairway, there was a low hanging tree at mid-fairway in the area dividing the thirteenth and fourteenth hole. It was shaped like an umbrella, and the branches hung low enough for me to slide underneath without attracting too much attention. "George, I am going for it."

"For what?"

"I am going to do it under that tree."

"Are you serious?"

"I am dead serious, but I need toilet paper."

"Well, don't look at me."

I ran to my golf bag—nothing except my brand new Titleist golf towel. It was a beautiful white towel with the script of "the greatest name in golf" not yet smudged by the slightest grass stain. But I needed it to wipe my ass. Oh well. This is a fucking emergency. I ran under the tree, grabbed a low-hanging branch for support and blasted away. I created the most disgusting pile of dung ever erected by a *Homo sapien*. I took one last look at my beautiful golf towel. It had cost me $14.99, and I hated to part with it, but what choice did I have? A golf cart was approaching from the adjacent hole. So I wiped my ass with the non-logo side and placed the towel, logo-side up, over the mound. That side of the towel was still without a single blemish. I was so ashamed, but what the hell. I felt great now, and I was only down one hole with five to play.

I won the thirteenth and I could sense George's confidence fading. My drive from the fourteenth tee, unencumbered by an ass full of shit, was a thing of beauty. It faded slightly to the right and landed in the fairway directly adjacent to the toilet tree. As we drove up to my ball, I saw a cart on the thirteenth fairway driving toward the tree. It was a father and son. The boy looked to be about twelve or thirteen. As they approached the tree, I heard the boy yell, "Look, Dad, a new golf towel!"

George and I instantly looked at each other. I could tell he was thinking what I was thinking. It was a terrible conundrum of mixed emotions. Should we yell out to warn him or sit back and enjoy the spectacle? The latter was chosen by default as the kid dove under the tree with both hands. He screamed, and his father ran in after him. I am sure he thought his son was bitten by a snake. When his father arrived he yelled, "Oh Shit!" as his son emerged from under the tree with both arms covered to the elbow.

It was one of those "had to be there" moments. We laughed out loud without let up for the next two holes. How fortunate could we possibly be to be standing right there when the trap was sprung?

It was time to get serious again about the game, but it wasn't long before another crisis developed. We had miscalculated how much time it would take to complete the round and drive to Raleigh to catch a plane back to Orlando. Missing the flight would force us to stay over Sunday night causing multiple other complications, both personal and business. To make matters worse, we had an octogenarian foursome ahead of us who were taking their sweet time. They were two old couples who lined up each putt as if they were at The Masters. The sixteenth hole was a par five, but George had an awesome drive that left him in the fairway about 250 yards out. The geezers were particularly annoying on this green, and finally, George pulled out his 3-wood. "Fuck it, I am hitting."

I wasn't overly alarmed as the shot was at least twenty-five yards out of his range, and maybe the sound of a ball landing close by would get these assholes moving. He then crushed the best 3-wood shot of his life. It was a screaming line drive about head-high heading straight as an arrow for the green. A hit would have been lethal, so we both yelled "Fore!" at the top of our lungs. All four of them hit the deck as if they were sailors on the flight deck of an aircraft carrier about to be strafed. It was a good thing they did, because the ball still had incredible velocity as it passed only about two feet over their supine bodies. They were clearly shaken, and when they finally picked themselves up, the two men waved their fists at us as they walked off the green.

By virtue of his superb shot, George took the sixteenth. He still led by one but we were now clearly pressed, and he knew that if we didn't finish the round he could not claim victory. He was irate, and his T-shot on the seventeenth sliced into the adjacent fairway. I took advantage of the miscue by making a cautious drive that landed in the middle of the fairway. As soon as I got in the cart, he started racing for his ball. He wanted to hit quickly while there was an opening between the foursomes that were actually playing that hole. He pulled out a 7-iron and said, "I am going to give you a break and lay up short."

"Maybe you should use an 8-iron," I said. "You can't risk hitting too close to those old geezers again."

"Yeah, I am sure you would love that," he snapped.

I stood behind him and was relieved to see that he was so determined to hit, he had lined-up the shot in such a way that I thought it would be impossible for it to land anywhere near the green. Wrong again. The shot took off in the direction I expected but then turned in mid-flight like a heat-seeking missile. It landed on the green within a few feet of one of the geezers, and this time they were really pissed. The two men left their wives on the green, jumped into one of the carts and headed straight for us waving their putters and screaming obscenities.

George knew he had no defense and started apologizing profusely.

"I'm sorry. I am very sorry," he said over and over. The geezers would not be appeased. They kept calling him a fucking asshole and other stuff and would not let up. Finally, George lost it. "Listen, you fucking old bastards; it's your own fault for taking forever to putt out. There are other people on this course trying to finish their round, but you are holding everybody up. I said I was sorry." He then raised his voice and screamed, "If that isn't good enough, then you can GO FUCK YOURSELVES!" They then took off as I am sure they were worried about what he was capable of if they continued to provoke him. In fact, they didn't even play the eighteenth. They picked up their wives and headed straight for the clubhouse. George was so agitated when he got to the green that he 3-putted, allowing me to take the hole. We were now tied with one hole to play.

It was my honor, and I again decided that caution was the best strategy. I hit a straight but short T-shot that traveled about two hundred yards before landing softly in the middle of the fairway. I would need an accurate 5-iron to hit the green from there, and George knew that my accuracy dropped off dramatically with anything longer than a 7-iron. He looked at me and sniffed, "You are fucking doomed." He then took a violent swing and crushed the ball. It flew straight for about two hundred fifty yards but then as luck would have it, slowly started to leak to the right. I smiled as it rolled into the rough, disappearing about eighty yards ahead of my ball. "Oh fuck!" he yelled.

"Gee, that's too bad George; it was such a great drive," I said with a sardonic smile.

He glared at me disgustedly as he got into the cart. We raced to my ball, and I got out and grabbed my 5-iron. I was startled when he took off as soon as he heard the club leave my bag. I yelled, "Where the hell are you going?"

"To find my ball," his voice trailed off as he drove.

George had broken a rule of golf etiquette as well as a common-sense safety rule by leaving me there. It is done all the time but typically not when you have to travel that far ahead. He wanted to win, and the anxiety of seeing his ball disappear must have clouded his judgment. I have two 5-iron shots, and I never know which one to expect. One is a beautifully arcing, high, 180-yarder that lands softly on the green, and the other is a shanked slice. George reached his ball and I heard him yell, "All right!" It must have been sitting up high enough for him to make an accurate wedge-shot which would likely win him the hole and match. This increased my sense of desperation as I took a determined swing. Unfortunately, the pressure must have gotten to me, because I ripped a high velocity slice that was heading straight for George. I yelled "Fore!" and George dove into the golf cart. Unfortunately for George, this cart had a space of two to three inches between the seat and seat-back. It really was a remarkable shot as the ball somehow managed to find an unobstructed space between our golf bags and between the seat and seat back. The space couldn't have been more than three-by-three inches. It was going full speed when it struck him square in the back. An Eagle would have been statistically more likely. George screamed, and I ran to him as fast as I could. He had a bad back to begin with, and I was truly concerned as he fell out of the cart onto the ground writhing in pain.

I helped him into the cart and headed for the clubhouse. That was it for golf. I offered to pay him on the bet as if I had lost, but he responded in a low raspy voice: "Fuck you."

As I approached the clubhouse, I saw the flashing light of a police car in the parking lot, and thought, *this is odd. Maybe one of those geezers had a heart attack.* As I got closer, I heard both of the old men yell, "There they are!"

At that point, a huge red-neck sheriff's deputy emerged from the car and yelled, "Get over here, boy."

Now this was great. George, who was the cause of the problem, was in too much pain to move so it was left up to me to appease these enraged old men, their wives and Sheriff Buford Pusser. The two old guys, seeing George bent over in pain, now wanted to kick his ass. I said, "Look, the guy just got hit with a golf ball, and he is in a lot of pain."

"Serves the bastard right," said one of the geezers.

Deputy Dog then demanded an explanation and said in a nauseating southern drawl, "They say you assaawlted them with a gaaulf baawl, not wooonce but twiiice. Is that truuuw?"

In panic, I started to think like a lawyer. "No sir. Assault requires intent, and this was an accident."

"Bullshit!" the geezers screamed in unison. "He shot for the green twice while we were still putting."

The deputy started to look at us very seriously. All I could think of was being thrown in some southern jail cell and having one of their red-neck, psycho inmates with three teeth force me to bend over and squeal like a pig like Ned Beatty in *Deliverance.* So I said, "Look. We are very sorry. I will pay for the rounds for all four of you." That shut them up, but it also cost me $160.

George watched me pay them off, and Buford Pusser seemed satisfied. All ended well, and we made our flight, but he never offered to pay even a portion of the $160. It took him weeks to recover from the deep bruise adjacent to his lower spine, and I sensed he felt I was responsible. It just wasn't worth debating the issues of why he rushed ahead and how he could possibly think I, in any way, intended to hit the ball in his direction. I let it go, but I still felt a strain between us that afternoon at the restaurant. He seemed to have little sympathy for my fear of losing Shmooky. In fairness, he had not met her. If he had, I am sure he would have understood.

8. Baby I Love You

Have I ever told you,
how good it feels to hold you?
—Barry, Greenwich & Spector
—As performed by Linda Ronstadt

After lunch with George and Larry, I went back to the office but couldn't concentrate on a thing. Janeka sensed my personal anguish but was also concerned that the work wasn't getting done. At 4:30 p.m., she stuck her head in to say goodbye but could not help reminding me.

"The *Revson* case is now set for trial in January, and Drew came by earlier to meet with you. Sam, I think he is concerned that you are not on top of things."

"That's ridiculous," I said defensively. "We still have more than two months to prepare. We will be ready."

"Okay, I am just reporting what I am seeing."

"Thanks, Janeka, but everything is under control. Good night."

Revson is the tractor-trailer versus Smart car case, and things were not under control. This was the highest profile case in the office, and what was left of my fading reputation depended on the outcome. The company had only reluctantly left the case in my hands. They wanted to send it to outside counsel, but I fought to keep it. They relented only when I agreed to have Drew co-counsel. Actually, other than the tasteless 1-800-EAT-SHIT joke, and my brief review of the file the night Shmooky made her surprise visit, I had barely thought about the case in weeks. The depositions of the grieving parents of the teenagers were quickly approaching, and I had not even begun to think about how to handle them, much less plan an over-all defense strategy. I knew Drew was losing his patience, but I couldn't concentrate. I needed to find out what had happened to Shmooky. If she went back to Ohio, that was fine. I just needed to know.

I was distraught when I returned home that evening. In the past, whenever I was miserable I could always count on Jen to make me feel worse, and more than one month after our divorce she still possessed that power. I checked my email and found the following under the heading: *EMERGENCY:*

Sam,

It is the fifth of the month and as I expected you are late with your first alimony check. I put up with your inconsiderate, intemperate, slothful, and revolting habits for twenty-seven years but now that I am free of you, I will no longer abide them for an instant. Your check will be hand-delivered by 9 AM tomorrow or I will have Mr. Spurlock immediately file an emergency Motion to Compel with Judge Smails. We both know that His Honor is so fond of you he will likely tack on attorneys' fees and costs. I could also move to have you held in contempt but what would be the point? If you were thrown in jail and spent the night with a bunch of other snoring, filthy, sots you would probably find the place to your liking and refuse to leave. I cannot subject our daughter to that kind of embarrassment.

It amazes me that Alexa still loves you when for twenty-one years you have placed her on your list of priorities just below Scotch, Steelers, Nittany Lions, golf, point spreads, Hooters, cigars, flatulence, belching, and scratching your balls.

Your check better be here. I am giving you fair warning. Don't fuck with me!

Jennifer McNamara (Notice that I am no longer using your dumb Goomba name)

P.S. John and I will be going away for a few days. I hear that Paris is lovely in the fall. I don't think it is too much to ask for you to stop by each morning and evening to walk Emma. You live only five miles away and with Alexa up at school, there is no one else the poor dog trusts. She is sixteen years old and almost blind, but her sense of smell is still very much intact. She apparently finds the stench of stale Scotch and the peculiar odor of your feet very comforting. Other than in your case, I hate to see an animal suffer. I have thought of putting the poor thing down but Emma was a birthday gift to Alexa when she was five and she is still very attached to her. I would hate to have to inform your daughter that you have refused this reasonable request.
Many thanks

Jen must be really excited about going to Paris, I thought, *since this is much less offensive than her usual correspondence.*

That night, I went to bed in a Scotch-induced haze. I had reluctantly agreed to meet with Drew to discuss *Revson* in the morning and drinking myself to sleep was a bad idea. I slept sporadically for a couple of hours, but at about 2:30 a.m., I woke up suddenly and my mind was filled with an overwhelming sense of panic. My apprehension was so intense, it was almost palpable. *She is downstairs and needs me now,* I thought. The premonition was vivid, and I could not escape the thought that her life was in danger at that moment. I quickly got up, dressed, and went downstairs. It was raining lightly, and Pedro, the concierge, asked, "Sam, meng where are ju going at this hour? The bars are closed meng; it is raining."

I appreciated his concern, but I was so agitated I felt like telling him to mind his own damn business. Since Pedro was a good guy, I resisted the temptation. "I just need to get some air. I will be right back," I replied.

I walked out into the damp, foggy evening. It wasn't raining hard, but just enough to be annoying as I headed toward Wall Street checking every door and alley along the way. The place was deserted with the exception of a couple of bartenders and waitresses walking to their cars. I turned down the side-street where I had found her weeks before and in the distance I could see the doorway but was alarmed at what appeared to be a street person hovering over something or someone. I quickened my pace until I saw a dark baseball cap lying in a puddle. With a feeling of both dread and relief I picked it up to confirm it was Chief Wahoo, and when I saw him grinning I ran for the doorway. There was Shmooky lying there. I couldn't tell whether she was asleep or unconscious.

The bum was looking through her backpack and after quickly checking her pulse I demanded, "Put it down!"

He looked at me with annoyance and said, "Fuck off! I was here first." I was in no mood to hassle with the bastard. Besides, he stunk of urine and cigarettes—not a combination I wanted to put my hands on. So I pulled out my .40 Glock, engaged it, placed the barrel on his temple and said, "I don't think you heard me. I said, put it down motherfucker!"

"Okay, man. Okay, just don't shoot. I am outta here," he pleaded as he ran.

I knelt down beside her and re-checked her pulse. She was alive but her hands were freezing and she felt feverish. I put her cap in the backpack, picked her up and held her tight against my chest. Such was the state of my physique that I strained to carry the tiny woman back to my building. She moaned softly as I held her. I had no idea she was injured. When I got her back, I kicked the door. Pedro came running. "Sam, should I call 911?" Her moaning had intensified, but I wasn't sure how to respond. Calling an ambulance would lead to the police and a lot of questions I probably couldn't or didn't want to answer.

"Not yet," I replied. "Let me get her upstairs. I think she will be okay. I will let you know."

"Okay, ju got it meng," Pedro replied.

I am sure glad I didn't tell him to fuck off earlier, I thought.

I put her on my bed and covered her in a blanket. I had no idea what to do so I went into the kitchen to boil water for tea and make myself another Scotch. If she was really sick, I would have a cab drop her at the emergency room at Orlando Regional in the morning and check-up on her later. When I got back, I sat next to the bed and watched her as she slept. Even in her disheveled state, she was still angelic. I thought of how content I was just to sit and look at her. I left briefly to check the water, and when I returned, I stood over her. I couldn't resist the impulse to stroke her cheek and hair and was a bit startled when she opened her eyes and looked up at me. She gave me a weak smile and said, "Hey, Shmooky."

I told her not to speak, but she turned out to be in a lot better condition than I had feared. It wasn't long before she started teasing me about how my wet hair exposed my thinning spots. My embarrassment turned to laughter as I continued to caress her while she giggled.

"Sam, why did you leave me in these wet clothes?"

A good question, I thought as I bashfully diverted my eyes. Removing her soaked clothes was not an option I had considered although it certainly would have made sense.

"Oh, I see," she laughed as she read my mind. "I guess you need candlelight and Dean Martin for that."

I enjoyed watching her laugh even if it was at my expense. Less than an hour earlier, I thought I had lost her. Now she was safely here and adorable as ever. I opened a drawer and playfully threw one of my T-shirts at her. It landed right on her face and she left it there as she continued to laugh louder. But when she went to the bathroom to change, I started thinking, and as hard as I tried, I could not control my concerned annoyance. "Do you know how worried I have been? What happened? Why did you break off contact with me without a word?"

"Please don't be angry. It's a long story, and I was afraid to tell you. I knew that you would find me, though."

Now puzzled, I said, "How could you be so sure? I had no idea what to do. In fact, I had given up and went downstairs just now on an impulse."

"That's what I mean; we are connected. You knew I was in trouble because you love me."

"What?" I gasped as if shocked.

"Don't try to deny it. I can tell."

I didn't respond. I was afraid to, but instead looked at her with an agreeing but equivocal smile.

"I need to tell you something Sam, and when I do, you may not want to see me anymore."

"There is nothing you could tell me that would make me send you away," I assured her.

She smiled and said, "Okay, here it goes. When I came down from Ohio, I briefly worked at Disney but found I could not make enough to live on."

"That's shocking, just shocking," I said sarcastically.

"Please let me finish. It got worse, much worse. The economy turned, and since I was the last hired, I was the first to be laid off. I was in deep trouble, with no money and no one I could turn to. That is when I met Eduardo. He was so nice at first, and he took me in."

"Well that should have been a red flag right there," I laughed.

"What?"

"I don't know. Maybe it's my own personal prejudice, but I think there is a rebuttable presumption that anyone with a name like Eduardo has to be an asshole. Obviously, he failed to rebut the presumption."

"Why are you making a joke of this?" she replied annoyingly.

The truth is, I really didn't want her to go on and making a joke of it was my typical way of avoiding unpleasant information. When I thought I had lost her, I created in my mind the perfect dream girl and molded her to fit this impossible embodiment of beauty and virtue. I didn't want to hear anything that would shatter this fantastic perception of her, but she was insistent so I said, "Oh, all right. I am sorry. Tell me everything."

"Sam, please don't get mad. I am not going to do it anymore. I did it a few times and it was horrible. So horrible, that I can't live with myself and have even thought of suicide."

Again, I desperately wanted her to stop and tried to diffuse it with a guess—a guess that I had a feeling might be wishful thinking—when I interrupted. "What are you talking about? Drugs? Because I have done a shit-load of drugs, and it isn't that bad. Sometimes I think back and consider my druggie years as the good ole days," I said laughing. "I love drugs."

"Would you shut the hell up," she snapped. "I wish it were drugs. Sam, listen to me, I am a prostitute and Eduardo is my pimp."

I stood there in silence for several moments and thought, *So this is the end of the mystery.* Shmooky was crying, and I am sure she felt like an eternity had passed waiting for my response. It was then that I realized just how much I loved her, because the first thing that hit me was that the shocking revelation didn't make a bit of difference to me. She was with me now, and my only thought was to take care of her and get her through this. I said, "Shmooky, that doesn't matter to me. I have done things in my life I am not proud of. The only thing that concerns me is your future. You know, Mary Magdalene was a prostitute but was Jesus' best friend."

I walked over to hug her but she abruptly pushed me away. "Didn't you hear me? I am a whore! I have no future."

"Shut up!" I shouted. She was shocked by my anger, and I immediately apologized.

"Look, you have been a prostitute for what, three months? Well, I have been an alcoholic for over thirty-five years. I won't throw stones at you if you don't throw them at me. How is that? Are we square?"

She smiled in agreement and extended her hand to shake mine. That is when I noticed the dark black and blue bruises on her arm above the elbow. As I tried to get a closer look, she pulled away and said pleadingly, "No, don't."

"Let me see it," I demanded.

She started to cry again and said, "I can't. Please don't."

"Let me see it, Shmooky," I insisted.

She slowly pushed up her sleeve revealing the dark, fresh bruising that extended all the way up her arm and included her right shoulder. My body filled with rage as I walked quickly back to the kitchen counter where I had left my Glock. "I am going to kill that son of a bitch!" I yelled.

She ran up to me and directed my arm back to the kitchen counter.

"Please put it down. You are scaring me."

"He is not going to get away with this," I snapped back.

"Sam, you have no idea what you are talking about."

At that point, I did what I always do when I am nervous or scared. I resorted to *Scarface* humor. Several years earlier, I had won a Tony Montana impersonation contest by default when my opponent, attorney Jake Callahan, backed out of the competition. I had never met Callahan but was told that if there was one guy in Orlando who could beat me, he was the man. It was a Friday evening happy hour event at The Star Chamber, a watering hole across from the courthouse frequented by lawyers. I had the whole movie memorized and was confident going in that he couldn't lay a glove on me. I think I intimidated him when I spoke to him on the phone the week before to issue the challenge. He was probing me to see if I was a serious opponent when he said, "Complete the following dialog: *You're here to watch my back, so watch my back.*"

Without the slightest hesitation I responded, "*Better than watching your front, let me tell you.*" There was a moment of silence on the other end of the line that told me he had realized he was out of his league. That Friday, the bar was full of people anticipating the showdown, but Callahan never showed up. I met him a couple of years later and have never let him forget his refusal to compete.

Holding my Glock, I looked at Shmooky and said, "I am Tony Montana, and when you fuck with me, you are fucking with the best."

She gazed at me in stunned disbelief. "You are totally out of your mind. This isn't funny."

"What? Tony Montana is always funny."

"Sam, please, you have no idea what he is capable of. He will kill you and then continue on with his day as if you were a mild inconvenience." She took the gun away from me and put it in the drawer. I wiped off a tear as I touched her cheek and said, "If he had touched your face, I would have killed him. I promise you that."

"He isn't that stupid," Shmooky replied. "I don't have a body. If he damages my face, I am worthless to him. He is all about money."

I learned that Eduardo is quite an imposing figure at six feet three inches, 250 pounds, and Shmooky was terrified of him. When he isn't running his crack and prostitution business, he spends most of his time pumping iron and practicing tae kwon do. He is rumored to have killed a prostitute and one of his competitors with his bare hands. He also never travels anywhere without an entourage of violent henchmen. The cops had an idea of what he was up to but could never seem to pin anything on him or infiltrate his operation. His prostitutes and crack dealers knew the consequences of betrayal.

The bastard sported a shaved head and an assortment of tattoos of chains, knives, and guns. The most notable were swastikas over each pectoral muscle. He raped Shmooky soon after he brought her in and continued to do so at every whim, keeping her in constant fear for her life. He took away any money he found on her and warned what would happen to her if she tried to run away. What options did she have? As Al would quip when faced with a betting dilemma, she must have felt like she was between his cock and a hard place.

A few hours before I found her, she was raped and beaten unmercifully as punishment for her lack of productivity. She fled into the stormy night without money and with only the clothes on her back. Since August, she was supposed to be spending day and night on the OBT, Orange Blossom Trail, but instead, hid as much as she could. It is hard for me to imagine what had been going through her mind—a woman with limitless potential relegated to selling her body with seemingly no way out. The thought of it disgusted me, but instead of finding Shmooky irretrievably repulsive, I was drawn nearer to her. I didn't know what to do about Eduardo, but she now had a place to stay and no need for money. She would be safe here.

Over the next couple of weeks, I was able to gradually nurse her back to health. The black and blue faded, and as she got stronger, she became more and more perky and provocative. She continuously peppered me with questions and observations, keeping me constantly on my toes. I was amazed when, no matter how hard I tried, I couldn't beat her at chess or even Trivial Pursuit, a game at which I was invincible. I was so happy to have her back in my life again that I was even able to refocus at work. I brought her lunch every day, and the evenings were spent talking and watching movies. We took turns watching each other's favorites and discussing them at length. She loved *The Godfather* and was fascinated by the deepening seven-hour saga through *The Godfather II*. She needed no prompting from me to conclude that as great as the original may be, the sequel is arguably better. I got hooked on *Breakfast at Tiffany's* and quickly noticed the striking parallels between my adorable Shmooky and Audrey Hepburn's portrayal of Holly Golightly: both of them captivating enigmas with boundless wit and charm to go with their stunning brown eyes. I didn't want it to end and one evening, I told her, "I want you to move in with me permanently. Please, the second bedroom is Alexa's, but she never uses it. Whenever she is in town, she either stays with her mother or with friends."

She hugged me and said, "I would love to, but I don't want to put you in danger. Eduardo is trying to find me, and when he does, he will hurt me again. If he finds out you are hiding me, he will hurt you, too."

"Fuck him," I replied confidently. "I am not worried. My only concern is you. I have only two conditions for you to stay here."

"Only two? I hope one of them is great sex. I am still waiting for you to make a move," she said with a laugh so cute it took all of my self control to change the subject.

"I want you to get your GED and then you are going to enroll in a SAT prep course. You are going to college."

"You're crazy! I am not going to college. Who is going to pay for that?"

"Don't worry about that right now. Let's get your high school degree, and then we will see how you do on the SAT. Once we get through that, everything else will take care of itself. I promise you."

She walked over and hugged me deeply. "You are willing to do all of this for me? Why?"

"Because I love you, Shmooky." It came out just like that, and for once, I didn't try to qualify it. It's the way I feel, and I can't hide it anymore. Her eyes widened in disbelief as I could see the emotion building in her face. It was clearly apparent that no man had spoken words of love to her since her father's death seven years earlier. Before she could cry, I pulled her close and said earnestly, "I have to confess something to you. I can't say I fell in love with you the first time I saw you." She gave me a bewildered look as I paused, "but definitely the second." Her eyes screamed with glee before I kissed her passionately for the first time since our initial awkward attempt during her surprise visit weeks earlier. I had never felt such inner joy in my life. I so adored her and didn't want to let go. When I tried to move away, she held on, reassuring me that she felt the same. When we finally parted, I looked into her eyes. She looked as if she could read my mind and gave me a look of encouragement. I couldn't. I loved her but knew this could go no further.

Sensing the tension, Shmooky immediately started teasing me. "Sam, this is going to work for you, too."

"Are you sure?"

"Oh, yes. You need someone like me to take care of you."

Having no idea where she was going with this, I replied defensively, "I have been alone for a while now. I think I can take care of myself."

"Dude, have you seen your refrigerator? You have two beers and mustard. You don't even have any Smuckers."

"Smuckers! Why would I have that?"

"Because it is yummy and made in Orrville, dummy."

I thought for a moment of how ridiculous the lifestyle of a divorced bachelor must seem to her. I had lived in the condo for over two years, and although it had state of the art appliances, I had never used the dishwasher, oven or microwave and had only used the stove to heat up an occasional can of soup. Either I had fast food, ate in restaurants, or brought in take-out three times a day. I looked into her eyes and earnestly said, "You can have one of the beers, but you may want to check the expiration date before using the mustard. She laughed and hugged me as I tried to think of how many years had passed since I felt this happy.

As I expected, Shmooky easily qualified for her GED and quickly enrolled in the SAT prep course. She showed her appreciation by applying for the first available test date and taking the accelerated course. Every moment not with me, she spent either studying or traveling back and forth from school. I drove her as often as I could, but she insisted she had no problem taking the bus. I had a problem with it because I knew Eduardo had his prostitutes and crack slingers on the street looking for her. She needed to be able to defend herself, so I called my cousin, Jack, to get his opinion on which weapon would be appropriate for her tiny hands.

Like Al, Jack was quite a colorful character. We grew up during the Vietnam debacle but rarely discussed it. Fortunately, the war had ended a couple of years before we graduated high school because we both knew that we would have had to go if it hadn't. It was the way we were brought up, and it was not subject to debate. I will never forget our last discussion on the topic because it has haunted me ever since. It was April 30, 1975, the day Saigon fell. We were watching the news when Jack said in disgust, "This is a disgrace."

"I don't care anymore that we lost," I replied. "It is the 58,000 dead, and for what?"

"That is exactly my point," he said earnestly. You don't ask young men to fight to the death unless the cause is unquestionably just and the commitment is 100 percent. To ask men to die for anything less is disgraceful." I agreed but had to wonder just how often in history have the issues been black and white, which only continued to beg the question in my mind regarding whether there is such a thing as a just war. As I was going through my own crisis in recent years, I found no respite when I came home from work and put on the news. The seemingly endless casualty reports from Iraq brought back all of the old memories. In a way, I felt ashamed for being so self-absorbed. My own troubles were trivial compared to what those kids were going through over there.

After Vietnam, I avoided anything that had to do with the military, but Jack was always fascinated with military history and weapons. He was also an expert shot and competed at the national level before age and fading eyesight caught up with him. You might say he was a little odd, but I never questioned his opinions regarding weaponry since he had spent his life selling and collecting guns, both modern and antique. Of course, Jen had a problem with him and simply referred to him as, "that gun nut." For many years, we rarely saw each other, but after my separation, I developed an appreciation for his outrageous sense of humor.

Jack lived alone above his gun shop on the south OBT. I hadn't been down to visit in several months, so he invited me over as soon as I called.

"Cousin Sam! Come on up to my private armory," he said as he gave me a warm hug.

He wasn't kidding. I usually visited him down in the store and had not been up to his apartment since he redecorated. The walls were covered with war art from old recruiting posters to reconnaissance photographs of Guadalcanal. He was also a published World War II historian, and his bookcases were full of memorabilia and books on weapons and military history. Like many experts, he took things a little to the extreme. His TV stood on an old ammo crate and his coffee and end tables consisted of sides of ammo crates held up at each corner by spent artillery casings. He had olive carpeting, a khaki covered couch and recliner and camouflage drapes.

I told him of my situation and he explained that with hand-guns, it is always a choice between stopping power and accuracy. Jack preferred Glocks for their durability and ease of handling. He told me that Shmooky should carry the highest caliber gun she can handle due to its superior stopping power. But he also warned me that the average handgun battle lasts 1.2 shots, meaning the guy that gets his shot off first and accurately, usually wins. That statistic argued for the smaller caliber weapon.

Years ago, Jack had me try the .45 Glock for my own use, but I had trouble controlling it. A .45 is a nasty gun that can put down even the biggest and meanest crack-crazed bastard with the first shot. Fortunately, Glock makes a .40 which gives up some stopping power but is much easier to handle. I have kept my piece under the front seat of my car for years. Of course, I hope I never need it, but I decided a long time ago that if the worst happened, I wasn't going out without a fight. It seemed that every couple of years, I read about some poor asshole with car trouble getting killed, execution style, along some dark stretch of Florida interstate. Florida cities are notoriously well-armed, with a Wild West mentality prevalent in many locales. There are neighborhoods in Miami that I wouldn't venture into without at least three clips. I am a lousy shot, but did I want to at least have a fighting chance or die suck-cuming on my knees, so to speak? For me the choice was easy.

Jack explained, "For a small woman like your friend, a 9 mm is the weapon of choice. There is no way she can handle your .40. There are smaller, less powerful handguns available, but I think she should be able to handle this one. It lists for $475 but you are my favorite cousin."

"I am your only cousin," I interrupted.

"You are my favorite cousin," he persisted, "so it's yours, out the door, for $400, and I will throw in a free box of ammo and gift wrap it. Is this for her birthday or are you saving it for Christmas?"

"Halloween."

"Cool. I have some great wrapping paper: black with orange dead bodies."

As I was leaving, Jack warned, "You know Sam, if Obama wins the election, he will probably reinstitute the ban on assault weapons. Can I interest you in an M-16? They are on sale."

I looked at him waiting for the punch-line, but after a few moments realized he wasn't joking. "I will think about it and let you know," I replied.

When I returned home that night, Shmooky was sitting in the bathroom starring into the mirror. "Hi Sam," she shouted as the door closed behind me. "I will be right out."

She never wore makeup and as far as I was concerned, didn't need to. The bathroom door was half closed, and when I glanced in as I walked by I was surprised to see her awkwardly trying to put on old makeup that had been left behind by Alexa. I immediately stopped and continued to watch her from outside the door from a position where she could not see me. I stood there mesmerized as she attempted to draw dark lines around her marvelous eyes. She appeared frustrated, and I was baffled until I realized that she did not see herself the way I saw her. In her haste, she smudged herself and then said, "Screw it," in exasperation before deliberately smudging the eyeliner below both eyes. I watched in amusement as she made funny faces into the mirror before announcing in a hilarious Cockney accent, "I am Ozzy Osbourne."

I couldn't help but laugh out loud. She abruptly turned toward me and must have realized I had been there for a while because I immediately sensed her embarrassment.

"Sam, do you think I am pretty?"

"Of course I do. Why?"

"Oh, I don't know. Back in high school, a couple of boys told me they thought I was cute, but no one ever said I was pretty."

"I think you are beautiful."

"Beautiful?" she laughed. "I think you are hallucinating from all of that Scotch."

I gently took her arm and turned her away from the mirror. "Shmooky, listen to me carefully. You are beautiful."

I saw a confused look of both disbelief and gratitude in her eyes. She may have been somewhat startled by my unsmiling sincerity because she swallowed hard before I said, "Hey, I brought you a present."

She had that look of a little child as I handed her the package. "What is it?" she asked, barely containing her excitement.

"Open it."

"It's heavy. It must be a hell of a rock. Are we getting engaged?"

"It's not a ring, but it should demonstrate how important you are to me."

She looked appalled when she opened the box. "This is your gun, and I don't want it," she protested in disappointment.

"It isn't my gun. I got you one that you can handle. I have a .40. This is a 9 mm."

"I don't care if it's a paper-weight. I hate guns, and I don't want it. It scares me just to look at it."

"Listen, Shmooky, you will be a lot more frightened if that bastard Eduardo finds you. Please, I am begging you to keep it in your backpack. You probably won't ever need it but wouldn't you rather be safe than sorry? I wish I could take you with me everywhere, but I can't. I will sleep a lot better knowing you can defend yourself."

She didn't respond but hugged me tight and said, "I am so scared."

"So am I," I replied. "But trust me on this. Okay?"

"Okay."

9. Never My Love

You ask me if there'll come a time
When I grow tired of you
Never my love, never my love
You wonder if this heart of mine
Will lose its desire for you
Never my love, never my love

—Donald & Richard Addrisi
—As performed by The Association

I loved living with Shmooky. She always seemed to know when to give me space and when I wanted her near me. On Tuesday and Thursday evenings, she had her SAT course and typically got home at about 11:00 p.m. I would usually be in bed with my door closed. Even though she was of age, I guess deep down I really was not sure whether it would be appropriate for our relationship to develop further. So even though I kissed and hugged her as much as I could, I always stopped just short of touching her intimately. It seemed she could read my mind, as she always knew when to stop and back away even though I, too, felt her passion.

One Thursday evening in October, she came home from her course and, as usual, found my door closed. She knocked softly and asked, "Sam, are you up?" After calling a few times and not receiving a response, she slowly opened the door and saw me sitting up but asleep with the TV on. My football betting notes were spread all over the bed, and my reading glasses were still hanging on my nose. She came over to tuck me in but just as she was about to turn off the television she heard the music of *VegasWorld,* the sports betting show. I had talked about the show endlessly, so she decided to step back and sit on the foot of the bed. At that point, the show's host introduced what everyone had been waiting thirty minutes to hear: the "release" of the Commissioner.

There he was in all of his glory: the finest picker in the land with his head taking up 75 percent of the TV screen. With his New Jersey accent, he started calmly but then quickly raised the decibel level until he was shouting uncontrollably, "I have analyzed the line. I have checked my sauwces and have tauwked to my peeps. Here's the release, the five-star lock of the century. This is free money so empty out your 401(k) (if there is anything left in it) and get down on the Dolphins over the Jets this Sunday." As the Commissioner continued to speak, you could see the veins popping from his forehead as his face turned a brighter and brighter shade of red. He continued, "Bret Faawvraa has not recovered since he was shown the door in Green Bay, but Chad Pennington has been reborn as if he met Jesus for lunch on South Beach. It is late October, but the game-time temperature in Miami is expected to be 89 degrees. Those slobs on the Jets offensive line will wilt in that cesspool. Tony Sporano has the Fins smelling the playoffs for the first time in five years. I know the man looks like he should be delivering pizza, but he has a factor! He will have his men motivated so lay the points and get down NOW! If you don't, you are an IMBECILE!" he shouted. Then, as abruptly as he started screaming, he suddenly became calm and solemn as he said, "This is the Commissioner, Al Goldstein. I have spoken."

Shmooky laughed out loud with a new appreciation for my obsession. I am sure she thought: *So this is the insane world of the Las Vegas bettor.*

She then turned off the TV and came to take the glasses off my nose. For some reason, she stopped herself and instead took off all of her clothes except her underwear and T-shirt and came into bed beside me. I then woke up and saw her lying next to me, watching me sleep. When my eyes opened, she smiled and said, "Hey, Shmooky" in a playful voice that immediately had me aroused. I then looked at the clock and said, "Oh shit! I missed the Commissioner." She said, "I heard him. The release is lay the points and take the Dolphins." I thought to myself momentarily and then agreed, *Makes sense.* I then asked her, "So what did you think of my old roommate, the Commissioner?" She laughed and said, "He's a wing-nut just like you."

She then moved closer, and as I put my arm around her, I noticed that she had virtually nothing on. At that point, my desire was uncontrollable, but I tried to start a conversation by asking, "So what else is up?" She smiled and touched me intimately for the first time and said playfully, "It appears you are, Counselor." She moved on top of me. I felt her warm soft skin, and at that point it was all over. I gently moved my hands over her body. She was so tiny, but I was more aroused than I could ever remember. She sat on top of me and removed her T-shirt. Her breasts were no more than an A cup but were soft and firm. Her nipples were erect and upturned. She then did what no other woman has ever done to me. She basically made love to me with her eyes. My heart was pounding as she slowly lowered herself on top of me. She was deliberate and almost solemn as she purposefully took complete control. I could not keep my eyes off hers as I softly touched her face and hair. It seemed to last forever and was so intense and powerful that when we finally simultaneously climaxed, I experienced a sense of complete ecstasy I did not know was possible. She would not let it end until we both collapsed.

She fell back against the bed as I flung my head back against a pillow trying to catch my breath. I looked over at her and gave an exhausted but satisfied look. She laughed and said, "What's up old dude, are you going to make it?"

"You are a monkey woman, a monkey woman," doing my best impersonation of Bill Murray as Carl Spackler. She giggled while playfully jumping back on top of me. "What is that from? You freak."

"*Caddyshack.*"

"I haven't seen it."

"You're kidding. There is so much I need to teach you about the classics."

"It's a classic? Who is in it?"

"Bill Murray, Ted Knight, Chevy Chase, Rodney Danger-field. I can't believe you haven't seen it," I replied incredulously.

"I know Bill Murray, but who are those other guys?"

"Ted Knight was in the *Mary Tyler Moore* Show."

"Who is she?"

"I can't believe this."

"Wait, Sam. Before you accuse me of being a moron, what year was *Caddyshack* released?"

"Uh, I think it was 1982."

"Dude. I wasn't born until 1988!"

"Shit. That's right. Should we be having sex?" I asked playfully.

"Yes, at least four times a day," she replied as she wrestled my arms down and kissed me deeply.

"I love you, Shmooky," I said with a voice of sincerity I never thought I was capable of uttering. She looked into my eyes, smiled and said, "I love you, too, Shmooky," before she put her head on my chest. Exhausted, I must have immediately fallen asleep.

The next morning, I felt her getting up and watched her walk out of the room naked. It was the first time I'd seen her body in partial daylight. She had the most incredible way of walking, and I was mesmerized by her cute little ass as she left the room. I thought to myself, *Maybe God has given her to me to compensate me for all I have lost. If so, I approve of the trade-off.* To experience this at fifty-two years old was just too wonderful to believe as my return to the single life had, until now, been very disappointing.

It is a truth that is patently unfair, yet still a truth. Men demand more than they are entitled to long after their own physical deterioration should be plainly obvious.

It is difficult to admit, but Jen had spoiled me. During our separation, friends had encouraged me to date and recommended that I try Match.com. Like all dating sites, age is the first factor under consideration. Naturally, a woman under forty will likely shop around in an age range that would exclude viewing the profile of anyone above the age of fifty. So at fifty-one, I had no luck "winking" at anyone under forty-five. I went out with a few women in their late forties and found them unappealing, especially naked. Maybe I am too picky, but my own flabby midsection and love handles notwithstanding, breasts of any size should be soft, but firm. They should also have a life of their own and not sag limply like a pair of over-ripe cantaloupes. Nipples should defy gravity, and always faithfully lead the observer to points north on the bedroom compass. The ass should be round and firm. It should not resemble the seat cushion of your recliner.

I had four partners who ended up in the sack with me. The first three had me thinking of an exit strategy while we were still deep in the throes of passion. I couldn't perform at all with the fourth. It was the first time in my life, and it scared the crap out of me. This experience had me driving like a mad man to the urologist the following day. I finally settled on Viagra, as Cialis and Levitra left me with a two-day hangover—much too high a price for mediocre sex. The whole experience was very frustrating, and after the initial three months, I let my membership lapse. Even at fifty-two, there were not many women over forty who could touch Jen. She was amazingly well-preserved, reminiscent of *Dorian Gray*—beautiful on the outside, but rotten to the core. Could she have sold her soul for a great rack?

Once that boundary had been crossed with Shmooky, there was no stopping us. We were like rabbits on steroids. We did it in the morning, at lunchtime, when I got home from work and again at bedtime. Four times a day, for days on end. It seemed her lust was even more insatiable than mine. I tried my best to keep up with this ninety-eight pound acrobat, but every romp ended with me frantically trying to catch my breath as if I had just gotten off a stress-test machine. She wore me out, but it was a good kind of hurt. She was also a bit of an exhibitionist and liked to walk around the apartment half naked, sometimes topless, at others bottomless, and occasionally, with nothing on at all except for her baseball cap. She only took that off to wash her hair. With all of this going on, I didn't need Viagra, although I am sure she would not have minded a four-hour erection.

I now know why many old people resist retirement and many more fight to stay out of nursing homes. It is the proximity to youth that preserves youthful thinking. It is why Bobby Bowden and Joe Paterno will not go quietly. Retirement is death to them. One morning, I was watching Sportscenter before leaving for the office. They were running yet another story about how Bobby and Joe have to go, and they showed the clip of Joe Paterno running from the field before halftime to avoid taking a dump in his pants. I agreed and yelled at the TV, "Retire you old bastards!" just as Shmooky walked out of the bedroom wearing nothing but a short, sleeveless T-shirt and panties. She walked up and gave me a hug and kiss before saying, "Yelling at the TV again? I am worried about you." I watched her walk out of the room while thinking how blessed I am. I then turned back to the TV and yelled, "You go, Joe!" I get it now. Shmooky had given me new life, as coaching maintains those two old geezers.

If there is a single word that defines the quality of a relationship, it is passion. Without it, couples are nothing more than roommates and merely having sex does not equate with passion. I hardly ever see real passion even among the engaged, who have presumably not yet been jaded by the cold reality of married life. I now felt it for the first time, and it is an uneasy combination of indescribable bliss and feeling unbearably vulnerable. She is all powerful and dominates every waking thought. I desire her more desperately than oxygen. She could squash me, but instead does all she can to reassure me. Whenever she senses my insecurity, she tells me repeatedly, "I am not going any-where. I will never leave you."

10. Ring of Fire

The taste of love is sweet
When two fiery hearts meet
I fell for you like a little child
Oh, but the fire went wild
                    —Carter & Kilgore
                    —As performed by Elvis Costello

I have lived my life expecting the worst, but always hoping for a reprieve. Things were going so well now that I actually started thinking about the future, rather than desperately trying to take life one day at a time. I was sick of that tired cliché. Taking shit one day at a time may divide it into digestible portions, but it is still shit. I had finally, grudgingly given in to the advice of friends and sought help when my marriage was crumbling. I found that talking to the psychologist was a lot more useful than the drugs. She gave me the sounding-board I needed to realize that the marriage was in fact irretrievably broken, and it was time to move on no matter what the cost. The anti-depressants may have served some purpose in the very beginning when I was so depressed I couldn't get out of bed, but as the months passed, I realized that they do absolutely nothing to help you move forward. I had made some progress, but the final divorce hearing presented the real danger of a relapse. Had I not met Shmooky on that terrible day, I am not sure that therapy or whatever amount of inner strength I may have been able to muster on my own would have saved me. As the song goes, I used to think I was a rock, an island, but few people actually are. The most important ingredient to prolonged mental health is the support you receive from your loved ones.

After meeting Shmooky, I threw the Xanax, Zoloft and Wellbutrin in the garbage, cancelled the next appointment with my psychiatrist, Dr. Weiner, and went off all of it, except the Lunesta, cold-turkey. They warn you not to do that. In fact, I was told by Dr. Weiner that I would need the medication indefinitely, and although he may be able to reduce the dosages, I should expect to remain on anti-depressants for the rest of my life. With or without Shmooky, that advice is a steaming pile of bullshit. However, I do love Lunesta. I take it about an hour before bedtime, and I am out until 7:00 a.m. I don't need an alarm clock, I have my bladder. Suddenly, without those mind-numbing drugs, I had unlimited energy without resorting to hourly doses of caffeine. With the addition of Shmooky's love, I was walking on clouds but made the mistake of assuming it would never end.

On a cool November morning, I was not able to drop her off at the SAT course so she had to take the bus. I didn't think anything of it as weeks had gone by, and the Eduardo nightmare was all but forgotten. Unfortunately for me, Shmooky ran into Priscilla on the bus. She was the one whore in Eduardo's harem that she had gotten to know and thought she could trust. She didn't tell her where she was living but just about everything else. When Priscilla reached her stop, Shmooky invited her to meet her for a drink that night at Jesse's and also added that her boyfriend works as a bartender there. It was a huge mistake since Priscilla was in Eduardo's doghouse, and she told all to get back in his good graces.

That night, Priscilla showed up at the bar and had a drink with Shmooky at about 9:00 p.m. "This is my boyfriend, Sam," said Shmooky. I extended my hand, but Priscilla seemed oblivious to it as she was checking me out. If I could read her mind, I am sure she was wondering what Sammie was doing hanging with an old goat like me and risking Eduardo's wrath in the process. I had my own thoughts about Priscilla. If she would take off the caked-on whore makeup and the silver ring in her left nostril, she would be a strikingly beautiful woman. What a shame. What the hell is she thinking? I looked over at Shmooky and thought, *Thank God she isn't into that look.* Shmooky shrugged and smiled before ordering. I served them a couple of margaritas. It was a Thursday night, and Florida State was playing on ESPN so the crowd was larger than usual. The next time I was able to look back in their direction, Priscilla had been sidetracked by a guy at the bar who was hitting on her. Shmooky waved and threw me a kiss before slipping out the door onto the crowded sidewalk and walked the two blocks back to the condo without getting spotted.

About a half-hour later Priscilla asked, "Where is Sammie?"

"She went home. She has a test in the morning," I replied.

Priscilla yelled, "Oh shit!" I thought it was a peculiar reaction, but she appeared to be drunk, and I was too busy to give it any further thought. I learned in bartending school to never discuss anything too serious with a customer. A customer may act as if they are interested in your opinion, but more often than not, you are risking a shitty tip, or worse, if you make the mistake of offering advice or an opinion they don't want to hear. When it comes to serving drinks there are only three wise men, and their names all start with *J*: Jack Daniels, Jim Beam and Johnny Walker. What I didn't know at the time was that Shmooky's narrow escape would now focus Eduardo's wrath onto me.

I left the bar at about 2:30 a.m. and took my usual route home. As I walked down Court Avenue, I noticed a car driving slowly toward me with its lights off. I should have taken off as fast as my exhausted legs could carry me, but instead, I stopped and watched as the car stopped and four very large men emerged and quickly surrounded me.

The bald guy said, "Hey asshole! You have stolen my property."

"Would you mind if I went home and got my Glock before we resume this discussion," I said, hoping for a laugh and a break.

"Oh, that's funny," replied the bald guy. One of the other thugs, sounding like he had an IQ of about 60, said, "He's a real funny guy, boss."

I hadn't given up on talking or joking my way out of it yet so I went into my Barack Obama routine: "Well then, why don't we all sit down and see if we can reach some common ground based on mutual respect for our differences and celebrate the value of our diverse cultural contributions to the great American family to which we all belong . . ." The next thing I remember was waking up in the ICU at Orlando Regional and looking into Shmooky's tearful eyes as I felt her hand gently squeezing mine.

They would have beaten me to death if it had not been for Devin, one of the servers at Jesse's. She was heading home when she drove up to the scene and laid on her horn until they stopped and fled. She called for help and then got out of her car when she saw who it was. She held my pummeled and bleeding body until the ambulance arrived. I had a concussion, three fractured ribs and fractures of the right cheek bone and left wrist, in addition to severe bruising to my left leg and ankle. There were also multiple internal injuries from their savage kicks. It is funny, although I don't remember doing it I must have instinctively protected my balls. It was the only part of me that didn't hurt, and looking at Shmooky filled me with an intense desire to make love to her right there in the ICU.

"Did you take the test?" I asked.

"Yes, but I am not sure how I did. I had a lot on my mind that morning."

"Like what?"

"You really don't remember a thing, do you? When I woke up yesterday morning and you were not there, I panicked. So many thoughts went through my mind, and I was crying. I thought you hooked-up with that cocktail waitress at Jesse's—

the one who is always flirting with you. I think her name is Devin."

"Devin flirts with me?" I asked incredulously.

"Sometimes, Sam, I wonder how you got as far as you have in life with such a weak grasp of the obvious. Anyway, I called your office, and they had not seen you. I didn't know what to think."

"Shmooky, you know I would never do that. I love you. I tell you that twenty times a day. Don't you believe me?"

"I do, and that is why I was able to pull myself together. I will never doubt you again."

In the morning of the third day of my admission, they moved me to a private room as my progress was more rapid than they expected. I attributed this to Shmooky's constant vigil. I was heavily sedated but was able to acknowledge and converse with the stream of visitors that started to arrive. Shmooky remained with me at all times, but always managed to quietly slip out of the room when a visitor entered. Early that afternoon, Jen and Alexa showed up. Alexa immediately came to me, but I could see Jen closely checking out Shmooky as she left the room. Alexa cried as she held my hand and told me how much she loved me, but Jen barely said a thing. I had the distinct impression that she came solely for the purpose of verifying I was really hurt. After thirty years, I was the Amazing Kreskin when it came to reading her mind. I knew her only real concern was whether there would be an interruption in her alimony checks.

While they were there, Larry the cop showed up. He came over and squeezed my hand while Alexa was with me and then went to the door to talk to Jen. I was interested in that conversation and knew Jen was never much for whispering. Larry asked her, "Jen, don't take this wrong, but do you know of anyone who would want to do this to him?"

"How the fuck should I know, Larry. He is an asshole, but that isn't grounds to kill him."

She paused before adding, "Is it?" as if she was hoping that Larry would say, "No Jen, the death penalty is certainly justified for anyone you think is an asshole."

I chuckled to myself, knowing Shmooky was listening to this. She always thought I had to be exaggerating when I described life with Jen.

It didn't take long for Shmooky to figure out that Priscilla had betrayed her, and the beating had really been intended for her. She knew exactly who attacked me but couldn't prove it and had no intention of telling anyone. When Larry said goodbye, she stopped him down the hallway and introduced herself.

"Oh, so you are the famous Sammie. Boy, does Sam have a crush on you," he said flirtatiously.

"Larry, I am really scared. I will be living alone until Sam gets out of here. He gave me a 9 mm Glock a couple of weeks ago, but I don't know how to shoot. Will you teach me?"

"Of course. I get off at 4:00 p.m. Meet me at the shooting range on John Young Parkway across from the jail."

When Larry left, Shmooky returned to the bench outside my room and waited for Jen and Alexa to leave. I pretended to doze off as the nurse arrived for the 3:00 p.m. shift change. I heard Jen ask her, "Who is that young woman waiting outside?"

"I don't know, but she has been here every minute since his admission."

"Well, can't you force her to leave?" Jen persisted.

"We asked her to leave last night, but she refused. We then called security to have her escorted out, and she started screaming like a banshee. So the doctor let her stay. Anyway, your husband seems to perk up when she is around. He almost died, you know."

"You mean ex-husband."

The nurse now seemed annoyed and replied, "Whatever."

Shmooky came in as soon as Jen and Alexa left.

"I cannot believe you married that woman. What were you thinking?"

"My face hurts Shmooky. Someday I will tell you the whole story, but for now I can only tell you what my therapist told me."

"What's that?"

"Your wife is a terrorist."

Shmooky took her shooting lesson more seriously than the SAT. Larry demonstrated the technique and then stood by in amusement as she went through the first box of shells. She looked adorable in her eye and ear protection as she practiced the stance, arm position and aiming techniques, as well as where to place her thumb. I always managed to forget that part, with the Glock's action giving me a painful reminder. She went shooting the next two days until she felt comfortable enough to complete her mission. She didn't tell me in advance, because if she had I would have tried to talk her out of it. The personal risk was far too great and there would be the unsettled issues that we would wrestle with later.

Eduardo had a large house in Pine Hills, a part of Orlando the locals referred to as "crime hills." He was very cautious and had surveillance cameras that provided a view of all approaches to the property. Having lived there, Shmooky was familiar with the comings and goings of his entourage of thugs, whores and crack dealers. She knew that if she remained patient, there were times throughout the day when he was alone for extended periods. She had to wait a few hours for the opportunity without being spotted, but when it came, she did not hesitate. She parked my car a few houses down and walked up to a front entrance strewn with weeds, beer bottles and garbage. Fortunately, it was a chilly morning so her over-sized sweatshirt would not draw his attention as it covered the 9 mm which was hidden in the front pocket of her jeans. She rang the door bell and waited.

"Well, well," Eduardo said as he opened the door. "You have a lot of guts showing up here, you little slut."

"Eduardo, please. I desperately need money, and if you help me I will come back and work the streets hard for you."

"Well then, get in here and suck my dick you little piece of white bread cunt. If you do a good job, I will think about giving you your old job back."

Shmooky walked in and followed him into the living room. "Is anyone here?" she asked, "because if there is, I would rather go to your bedroom."

"No one is here. Now get to work," Eduardo ordered as he unzipped his pants. "By the way, we had to teach that old bastard you have been fucking a lesson. Kicked his sorry ass real good. Must have been touch and go for a while, wasn't it Sammie? Heh, heh, heh."

As Eduardo pulled down his underwear exposing his erect cock, he continued to taunt her, "So I guess the old bastard is going to live, at least for now. I will have to pay him a visit once he feels good enough for another beating."

Shmooky smiled as she placed her hand in her pocket, slipped it over the handle of the Glock, and placed her index finger on the trigger. If she had any lingering doubts about whether to go through with it, Eduardo's last threat ended it.

"It does look like he will live, but you will never be around to hurt him again," she said matter-of-factly as she pulled the gun out, stepped back and aimed it carefully. Eduardo yelled, "No!" as she put the first of four rounds into his chest. She then stepped closer and put a fifth shot into the middle of his forehead as he lay bleeding. As she put the gun back into her pocket, she walked up and looked down over his lifeless body before reaching back deep into her throat to collect enough phlegm to spit in his face. Years of watching baseball taught her the technique of spitting like a man, and she was satisfied with the huge loogie she left hanging from his nose.

Shmooky came back to the hospital and closed the door behind her. She didn't have to say a word. I could tell instantly by the look in her eyes that something terrible had happened. I sat up in the bed and listened in stunned silence as she told me the story. Her main concern was what I thought of her as she didn't seem to have the slightest bit of remorse. "The bastard deserved it. I couldn't let him get away with almost killing you. Not to mention all of the times he beat and raped me. There is no evidence linking him to the attack on you, and when the time was right he would have come after us again. He would have never left us alone. What choice did I have? It was self-defense and defense of a loved one. Wasn't it?"

When I didn't give her my immediate and enthusiastic approval, I knew that she regretted telling me. As much as I wanted to ease her fears, I didn't know what to say. From a purely legal standpoint, it could not be justified, but that didn't necessarily make it wrong. The practicalities were exactly as she described. We would be in constant danger as long as he was out there. I couldn't help but admire her courage. I probably would have continued to equivocate on how to deal with Eduardo as long as I thought there were any other possible solutions. To Shmooky, his continuing threat meant this was a fight to the death. She saw no alternatives and no reason to delay taking action.

Still waiting for my response, she pleaded tearfully, "Sam, please, tell me what you are thinking. Please."

"This is all my fault," I replied. "I gave you the gun. Three weeks ago you were afraid to even look at it. Now you have become a miniature Terminator."

"That isn't funny," she replied in an exasperated tone.

"Shh. Come closer," I replied. I leaned toward her and gently kissed her lips. I then looked into her misty eyes and barely above a whisper solemnly said, "Listen, Shmooky, I love you—now more than ever. You did the right thing but we can never discuss this again. Never. No matter what happens in the future, this will always be our secret. It's a secret I will take to my grave. Do you understand?"

"Yes, completely." She then took off her shoes and climbed into my bed. She put her head on my chest and hugged me. The hug was soft as she carefully avoided disturbing the various wires, tubes and IV lines, while at the same time I couldn't help but feel her desperation, as if the hug was for dear life. When the nurse came in, I gave her a look that she immediately understood. She left the room allowing Shmooky to stay with me all night.

Eduardo, in fact, would have gotten away with it since I couldn't positively identify any of my four attackers. The police had me review hundreds of photos in the hospital, but none of them could jog my memory. Devin was too hysterical when she came to my aid to remember a thing. She was unable to accurately describe any of them and couldn't even identify the type of car they left in. In a way, she was more traumatized by watching the beating than I was receiving it, since I couldn't remember any of it.

Shmooky knew she had a good chance of getting away with it. She was aware from her time living there that his surveillance system did not videotape because he feared the police could use it as evidence against him. The cops had been trying to nail him for years and would consider this the perfect ending to find him sitting there with his pants down at his knees. Any number of whores from Eduardo's stable would have had a motive to whack him. He mistreated all of them. She rightly guessed that any investigation would be short and inconclusive. Nobody cared. It was good riddance for all concerned.

Al made a surprise visit the day before I was discharged. I was so moved that he traveled across country in the middle of the football season that I cried and then laughed when he said, "Holy shit! You look like you were in a Pier 6 brawl and were the only asshole without a foreign object."

"Yeah, and my face was a crimson mask," I quipped ala Gordon Solie.

"Hey, where is this little shiksa you have been telling me about? And how the hell can you stand this humidity? It is November for Christ's sake!"

"She will be back in a while. How were you able to leave Vegas?"

"It wasn't easy. When I got off the plane, I had about thirty cell phone messages. I am going to Miami later to hang-out for the weekend, see the Fins game, and meet with my sources. I am even hoping to get into one of The Tuna's press conferences. Maybe I can get him to have one of his famous meltdowns. I told the casino I am on a business trip, and they are cool with it. Besides, I know I said I couldn't, but I have decided to come to Alexa's wedding. I am going to make a swing up the east coast over the next couple of weeks to research first-hand the teams that appear to be play-off contenders."

"That's great! What changed your mind?"

"You getting your ass kicked. I also want Jen to know that she can't intimidate me. She may have won that loser-leave-town match ten years ago, but if she tries to screw with me this time, I will have my steel cage match. I have been working out."

"Awesome!" I replied. "If you have any trouble, you can always tag-up with me, and we can double-team her on the ropes."

"What a great life you have," I said admiringly.

"It sounds better than it is," Al replied. "I am under an awful lot of pressure. Millions of dollars are on the line every weekend. Listen, my offer is still open. Quit that lousy job and move out to Vegas. You can bring the little shiksa with you. Out there no one is going to notice the age difference. Hell, you could be banging your pet Doberman and nobody would give a shit. Nevada is amazing." I laughed, but Al seemed humorless when he said, "Listen, Sam, I have to go but I want you to seriously think about moving. This attack should tell you something. It is time for a big change. So talk to the little shiksa and we will discuss it when I get back for the wedding."

"Hey Al, when you are down in Miami check out this radio sports talk show host, "The Mad Dog" Jim Mandich. He is hilarious and has an original and unique style that is every bit as entertaining as Gordon Solie's. You are going to want to call in and unload on him."

"I will check it out. See ya."

It wasn't only Al's invitation to Nevada that had me reassessing my life. It was clear to me that other than my small group of loyal friends, I only cared about three people: Shmooky, Alexa and my partially deaf octogenarian mother. Shmooky had proven how much she cared, over and over. It was Jen's influence on Alexa that had me worried.

In the afternoon of the day before I was discharged, Alexa came by to visit. I was relieved to see that she did not bring her mother with her. Shmooky had gone back to the condo for a couple of hours and would not return until dinner. This would give us the opportunity to finally have a quiet father-daughter talk.

"I am looking forward to your wedding. It's only three weeks away. Are you nervous?"

"Very," Alexa replied. "Are you going to be well enough to walk me down the aisle and give me away?"

"Of course. I will do it even if I have to crawl. But I won't. My legs feel pretty good. I should be able to get by with a cane. I am really looking forward to it. You are my beautiful daughter, my only child. I will spare no expense to give you the best blow-out party. I did notice, however, that out of a guest list of two hundred your mother allotted only two tables, twenty seats, for my friends and family."

"I know, Daddy, but Mom says that you have no family other than grandma and Uncle Jack, and all of your friends are assholes and alcoholics."

"Well, you can tell her that her friends and family don't need to drink to be assholes," I replied in an irritated tone. "Look, I really don't care about the guest list except for one. She is my best friend, a real friend, not a golf or drinking buddy."

Alexa took my hand and said, "That is fine. Of course she is invited."

"There is just one possible problem," I warned. She is twenty but will be turning twenty-one in less than three months."

"You are really sick, you know that, Dad!"

"Alexa, I am begging you not to make an issue of this. Besides, she is of legal age. What is your frigging problem?"

"But Daddy . . ."

"Listen to me carefully," I interrupted. "The wedding is already paid for, and I would never take that away or do anything to embarrass you. But if you snub her, I will give you away and skip the reception. I am dead serious. So think about it. Other than you, Sammie is the most important person in the world to me."

"So her name is Sammie? How convenient. Even you couldn't forget that."

"Alexa . . ."

"Oh, shut up, Daddy. I will talk to you tomorrow."

She quickly kissed me and left. I took that as a *yes* and was satisfied.

Alexa had the extra key to the condo and went straight over. She gave Shmooky a surprise knock at the door. When she opened it, she immediately felt judgmental eyes penetrating the force field she always maintained to protect herself from women like Alexa. Shmooky had an abundance of self-confidence that wasn't always evident on the surface, but felt inadequate and somewhat ashamed in her ragged jeans and T-shirt as she invited Alexa in. Alexa had an exotic, striking beauty as she was lucky to inherit only the best features from both her parents. She never ventured outside without looking perfect with her long flowing dark hair, blue eyes and the flawless body of her mother always dressed in the latest designer fashions. Her mother had trained her how to shop since she was a toddler.

"Alexa, I am Sammie . . ."

"I know who you are. I saw you at the hospital," Alexa replied, cutting her off.

Shmooky thought she was in for an unpleasant confrontation, but instead, Alexa's demeanor changed as she reached out and gently took hold of her hand. "I don't know what is going on between you and my father, and I really don't want to. Frankly, the thought of it grosses me out. But you apparently make him happy, so that is fine with me. All I have done since my parents' separation is worry about him. His drinking, gambling, cigar smoking . . ."

"I am really trying to help him," Shmooky started to explain.

Alexa cut her off again and said, "I know you are, and I am grateful." Alexa pulled her over and gave her a hug before saying, "See you at my wedding," as she walked out the door.

11. Total Eclipse of the Heart

Once upon a time I was falling in love,
Now I'm only falling apart.
There's nothing I can do,
A total eclipse of the heart.
                    —Jim Steinman
                    —As performed by Bonnie Tyler

It is amazing how quickly they discharge you these days. If it was up to my health insurer, I would have been dumped at the curb from my wheelchair with the IV line still in me—those heartless, greedy bastards. On the day Shmooky brought me home, the news arrived and as much as I knew she was brilliant, her 1350 SAT score was about one hundred points higher than I thought possible. We celebrated that night, but as I slowly regained my health over the next few days, a terrible reality started to grip me. I felt older, and although I was told that I could expect close to a full recovery, our age difference became more and more glaringly apparent. I was fifty-two and had come very close to death. Even before the attack, I had almost constant low back pain and needed medication to control my blood pressure and cholesterol. She had her whole life ahead of her. I agonized over what I should do but ended up doing what I always did when I needed help. I called Janeka and asked her to meet me for lunch the following day.

As much as Janeka always liked to torment me, she seemed genuinely concerned when she saw me approaching her table walking with a cane. She got up and hugged me before we sat down to discuss my return to work and the status of my cases.

"There is something I must tell you about *Revson*," she said nervously while carefully studying my face.

"They have taken the case from me," I replied with resignation. I was confident I knew the company's move before they made it.

"How did you know?" Janeka said with surprise.

"I have been in this business a long time. They didn't want me on the case to begin with, and my misfortune was the excuse they were waiting for."

"You are now sitting second chair to Drew. Are you upset?"

"No, not at all; it is a good move to replace a lawyer that no longer gives a shit with one that does."

Janeka quickly changed the subject and started rattling off, alphabetically, the status of all sixty of my remaining, fascinating fender-benders. I was amazed at how she could recall the nuances of each case. I hadn't been able to do that in at least a decade. I needed that brain space for point spreads and drink recipes. I couldn't have been more disinterested. In any event, what did it matter? Ninety percent of the plaintiffs in my cases were not injured at all, and in regard to the remaining 10 percent, I had no qualms about paying whatever it took to make them go away.

I watched Janeka talk and talk, but I really wasn't listening. I would occasionally nod in agreement while my mind continued to drift back to Shmooky, my love. She was all I could think about, and since the attack, I had difficulty focusing on anything else. I could not bear to be away from her for so much as an hour. As I sat there, my body was beginning to ache as I was no longer used to sitting in a straight-back chair. All I wanted was to return home to cuddle with her on the couch. I now felt completely dependent on her for my happiness and in a way, felt that I owed my rapid recovery to her, if not my life. If there was a chance to slip away, she had it when I was bed-ridden. No one would have judged her harshly. Who could blame her for ditching a now crippled old man? But she stayed and never left my bedside.

Janeka didn't like being ignored and finally said, "Look Sam, it is time to move on from all of this. I know that child is living with you, and I know you don't want to hear it . . ."

"You are right, I don't. Janeka, listen to me. I love her, and I am going to take care of her as long as she needs me."

"Who is taking care of whom?" Janeka shot back. "Sam, you have a good heart, but you are a screw-up. It's not your fault; it's what you do."

"You are really pushing the envelope with me. I know we have been friends a long time, but I am asking you to back-off."

"Sam, when you have let your conscience guide you, things have always worked out for the best. Haven't they? You are letting your emotions control you. Are you listening, Sam?"

"Yes," I replied. "But you know, about twenty-five years ago there was a TV show, *The White Shadow*. It was about a white basketball coach who coached a predominantly black high school team. Off the court, he was always trying to keep them out of trouble. You know—the white man's burden and all that—a condescending premise for a TV show if ever there was one. Well, anyway, you have become my frigging "black shadow," always trying to get me to do the right thing—whether I want to or not. You are really a pain in my ass."

"Sam, you know I am right, and you know what you have to do. Sure, it is going to hurt, but let her go, Sam. Do the right thing and let her go."

"She won't go. You don't know her. She will never leave me."

"Then send her away. This has to stop now. Sam, that girl is twenty. Send her away now, before she ruins her life."

I knew she was right, but every time I came close to admitting it to myself, my mind quickly shut down. It was a subject that I chose to avoid. Janeka knew I was angry with her. It wasn't the first time she had one of her "come to Jesus meetings" with me. When we got up to leave, she gave me a deep hug, which I accepted and returned. I knew that other than Shmooky and Alexa, she was one of the few people on the planet who genuinely cared about me. "I will be back to work after the new year," I said as we parted.

"Take care, Sam. I will see you at the wedding. Think about what I have said."

I half-smiled and turned away.

As soon as I got back upstairs, I decided to get things moving while there was still time. I waited until she went down to the gym to work out to fill out the online application to Ohio State. With her score, I received notification within two weeks of her early acceptance to start in January, less than four weeks away.

I knew I had to talk to Shmooky, but I had to get us both through the wedding first. I wanted her to look her best and noticed that the only jewelry she wore was her mother's wedding ring. I bought her a diamond and gold floating heart necklace.

"I am giving you your Christmas present early," I informed her matter-of-factly.

"Really, what is it this time, an AK-47?" she replied sarcastically. I handed her the box, and the look on her face when she opened it made me realize that I may have made a mistake. I deliberately did not get her a ring so as to avoid any misunderstanding, but Shmooky didn't take it that way. She saw the necklace as a symbol of my undying love, which it was, but also as confirmation we would marry, which was not my intention.

As much as I found her incredibly adorable, I was still shocked to see her on the day of the wedding. Alexa had taken her to buy a dress, shoes, purse and all of the accessories. In close to four months, I had never seen her out of her usual attire. She wouldn't allow me to return to the condo until she got back from having her hair and nails done. My jaw dropped when she walked out of the bedroom. It was a complete Cinderella transformation. "Where is my cute little tomboy?" I asked.

"Right here. Sam, don't get me wrong. I appreciate all of this, but this isn't me."

"I know, Shmooky, but just this once, I want to walk into that reception with you on my arm and watch all of Jen's family and friends go out of their fucking minds. And they will."

"Of course, my dearest, I will do it for you. After all she has put you through, you deserve the perverse pleasure of walking in with a twenty-year-old. I also promise to behave. I won't drop any F-bombs or flip Jen off."

"You don't need to flip her off, my darling. Your presence will be the ultimate *fuck you!*"

"Hey, Sam."

"Yes, sweetheart."

"Once we are done with this, I am going back to calling you 'old dude,' and you must promise to go back to calling me Shmooky. I can't handle this dearest, darling and sweetheart horseshit."

"Yes, my love."

I arrived at St. James Church with Shmooky, and her entrance resulted in the predictable reaction. We were running late and the church was full. Everyone stopped talking and turned around as I entered with her. I handed her to one of the ushers who happily escorted my petite, angelic-looking lover up to the front row to sit with Al and my mother. I proudly walked Alexa down the aisle as 90 percent of the congregation shot daggers at me. It was as if they felt I didn't have the right to give away my own daughter. I knew Alexa didn't feel that way, as she smiled all the way down the aisle. I looked at the few people who gave me positive vibes and ignored the others.

At the reception of two hundred at the Dolphin Resort, my friends sat at two tables that were strategically placed by Jen to be farthest from the main table and dance floor. She actually did me a big favor as it made it easier for me to avoid her pompous and judgmental crowd. My mother was all the family I had, and at eighty she was still hanging in there. She had slowed noticeably in the last couple of years, but she didn't flinch when I introduced her to Shmooky. "It is a pleasure to finally meet you Mrs. Russo. I am Samantha Wilenski."

"What a lovely dress," my mother responded.

I looked at Shmooky and said, "Samantha?"

"That *is* my name," she replied.

"Well, I know, but you have never used it."

"That is because I have always hated it, and if you start calling me that I will put a laxative in your Scotch bottle."

Shmooky was called over by Al as my mother asked, "Who is she, Sam?"

"Just a friend," I replied evasively.

"A friend of Alexa's?"

"No. Of mine."

"Oh. Well, she is very pretty."

"I know, mom," I replied. I have no idea what she was actually thinking, but she tactfully avoided asking me any further questions.

What a difference with Al! Whereas Jen and Al couldn't stand being in the same room together, he immediately hit it off with Shmooky. She was able to do an accurate imitation of him making a "release" on his TV show that had him bent over laughing. They spent dinner talking about the Browns and Buckeyes, and afterward Al asked, "Sam, where did you find that little shiksa? Whatever you do, don't ever let her out of your sight."

Jen had placed George and his wife, Andrea, at a table in a more desirable location, but he spent much of the time down in our little corner of the reception hall. He asked, "Do you mind if I sit down here for a while? You people are making so much noise, I feel like I am missing the party."

"I am sure I will hear about it," I replied. "This is the alcoholic section, and you are welcome."

With Shmooky, Al, Larry and his latest girlfriend, Janeka and her husband, Drew and his wife, Cousin Jack, the gun nut, and his floozy girlfriend, as well as other assorted characters, we made quite a scene. Jen's family looked on in disgust, but they had no idea what was coming. The highlight of the evening was when Shmooky approached the band leader and asked him to play *Conga* by Gloria Estefan. What had been a very dignified reception erupted as Shmooky and Al led the conga line in a wild serpentine romp through the reception hall. Even my mother joined in. It took a couple of minutes as Jen, her family and friends looked on in stunned silence, but when Alexa, her husband and the entire wedding party joined the line almost everyone else followed. The band extended the song another fifteen minutes until people started to fall off the line in exhaustion. It was gratifying to me when, by the end of the evening, I had been approached by George, Janeka, and even Alexa letting me know how much they adored Shmooky and completely understood why I was so captivated by her.

The climactic event of the evening was when I danced with Alexa before handing her to her husband. I then pulled Shmooky onto the dance floor. While all eyes were initially on the bride and groom, there were many curious looks focused on us.

"Sam, everyone is looking at us."

"That is understandable. You are so beautiful. I am the luckiest guy in the world. I have two beautiful women in my life."

"Your ex is freaking me out. She keeps talking to people while looking over and pointing at us. Doesn't she know that's rude?"

"Good. You are having the desired effect," I laughed. "Just ignore her, and remember she is only doing what she has been trained to do."

"I know, terrorize the rest of us," she giggled.

I could see the mischievous wheels turning in her head before she said, "Hey, Sam."

"Yes, my love."

"Let's dance like they did in *The Godfather*." She placed her feet on top of mine as she smiled and hugged me tight. I looked into her eyes as I thought nothing could be more precious than she was to me.

It was a wonderful evening. Unfortunately, I had to face reality again, and Shmooky's future had to be resolved. There would never be a good time to discuss the problem with her, but it had to be done. So a couple of days after the wedding, I awkwardly raised the issue.

"Shmooky, let's talk about Ohio State."

"I am not going to Ohio State. I am going to apply to UCF. I told you, I am not leaving you," she protested.

"Nothing would make me happier than to be with you for the rest of my life, but that's just it. Hasn't it occurred to you that even if we got married tomorrow and immediately had children, I would be in my seventies when the first one left for college? The men in my family don't make it to seventy. My father didn't even make it to sixty."

"I don't care, Sam. I don't want to have children."

"Yes, you do. You told me so, shortly after we met."

"Why is it you can remember a comment I made four months ago but can't remember what I told you yesterday?"

"Ah, ha! You see, you are now getting the picture."

"Picture of what?"

"Your future."

"My future?"

"Your future if you insist on living with an old man. You see, I can quote my favorite lines of Oscar Wilde, word for word, but can't remember what I had for breakfast. Here is an example: *To get back my youth I would do anything in the world, except take exercise, get up early or be respectable.*"

Shmooky laughed, "That is why I fell in love with you, Sam. You are so charming."

"You call it charm. Everyone else calls it dementia."

"It doesn't matter. I changed my mind. I don't want to have kids," she replied. Now crying, she pleaded; "Sam, please, I love you. Don't do what I think you are about to do."

"Shmooky, I am thirty-two years older than you. I am an old man, and since the attack, I really do feel like one. I am in pain every day. You deserve so much more than spending your youth taking care of a train-wreck like me. You may think you love me now, but . . ."

She rushed toward me and hugged me, before pulling her tearful face out of my chest. Now pleading, she said, "Sam, please listen to me. When your hair turns white and falls out of your head, when your blue eyes—those deep blue, kind eyes that stopped me in my tracks when I saw you alone in that restaurant four months ago—fade to gray, I will still love you."

"You don't know what you are saying," I coldly replied.

Now visibly angry, she pushed me away and threatened, "You can throw me out, but I will be right downstairs waiting for you every day until you change your mind."

"But what about your future?"

"My future is with you."

"Shmooky, listen to me. I love you more than I thought it was possible to love anyone, but I thought about it long and hard when I was in the hospital. How selfish it would be of me to try to keep you. I want you to meet a boy your own age when you are in college, get married, and have a family while pursuing your career. You are brilliant, beautiful, and talented. You have your whole life ahead of you," I said earnestly.

"I don't believe in that American dream of a house in the suburbs with a white picket fence, two kids, a dog and a mini-van, bullshit," she said dismissively. "There is only one true love, one soul-mate for everyone. I found mine, and you know I am yours. I have told you over and over." She cried, "I am not going anywhere," as she ran into the bedroom and slammed the door.

Her reaction was predictable, and I felt intense guilt, especially after all she had done for me while I was recovering from the attack. After that gut-wrenching conversation, it was apparent that all logical arguments would fall on her preciously soft and perfectly formed deaf ears. Since that strategy would not work, I concluded that I was left with no choice but to do what I have been trained to do: Lie like a motherfucker. There is a rule generally unknown outside my profession that is never discussed within it. You see, since I went to law school and am still an upstanding member of the Bar, I cannot be called a liar. In my wretched business, use of the word "lie" or "liar" is strictly prohibited. A lawyer may make a misrepresentation in the process of zealously advocating his client's case. He may add mitigating facts that never existed or omit inconvenient facts that could shift the preponderance of evidence against him, but he never lies. Use of the term to describe one of your brethren would bring the wrath of the court down on you instead of the liar. You also can't call another lawyer's case a lie. Parties and witnesses have poor memories or misspoke or lack veracity, but you can't scream, "Liar!"

A lawyer may fabricate, fib, equivocate, prevaricate, fudge, deceive, delude, dupe, fool, hoodwink, misinform, misguide, misrepresent, misstate, distort, garble or dissemble, but do not accuse him of lying. Bill Clinton never lied. There really are many definitions of the word *is*. Volumes have been written on existentialism, which is a philosophy that is essentially an attempt to define that two-letter word. Whether he had sex with that woman is also subject to debate. Having sex is difficult to define. I know what it means to me, but I have known men who consider a visit to a titty bar as a sexual act akin to infidelity, as insane as that may sound. Even Richard Nixon is not called a liar. The history books only refer to a "cover-up." You must also be aware that if you accuse the liar of lying, be prepared to be called a liar yourself for having the temerity of exposing the lie. If you persist, they will not stop with the issue at hand but will scour the record of your entire existence to find something, anything that will allow them to yell: Liar! Hypocrite!

But as a highly trained professional liar, I digress. I am going to lie to Shmooky, the love of my life, because—get ready—it is for her own good. There is no better justification for a bold-face lie than to be able to say your motives are pure. It is merely a "white lie." There are many definitions of a white lie. It is a common notion that a white lie must involve a trivial issue or some unimportant fact. Not necessarily. A white lie can also involve a critical matter. The key is the liar's intent. If the lie is told diplomatically, or it is well-intentioned or told to be polite, tactful or to avoid injury or hurt, it can also be considered a "white lie." Referring to the previous example, Bill can legitimately claim his lie was a "white lie" even though it was not a trivial matter because of the greater goal of avoiding injury to Hillary and Chelsea. So as long as you have altruistic intent, you can lie your ass off, and that is exactly what I am going to do.

The next day, I raised the issue again, this time with an elaborate prevarication ready to be told in all its minute detail. "Shmooky, we have to resolve the issue of your future and, before you get upset, hear me out. I have been fed up with my career for a long time. What if I told you that I want to leave Florida and my law practice to move to Columbus, Ohio?"

"Are you serious?"

"Absolutely. I love you and can't live without you."

"But what about your obligations down here?"

"I can't think of a better way of screwing Jen than to stop working. They can't take from me what I don't have. I will abandon the condo. She can have it, and if she doesn't want it, the bank can foreclose. I really don't give a shit. My credit is destroyed anyway. We can rent a place near campus. I will tend bar and start the career I have always dreamed of as a fiction writer while you are in school. What do you think?"

"I think it sounds wonderful. Are you really prepared to do this?"

"There is no question in my mind. I can't bear the thought of going back to work after the New Year."

Shmooky screamed, "Yes!" and flung herself in my arms. I held her close to me and stared into the empty space behind her. *I am a cad,* I thought. *Maybe, but there is no other way.*

"There is one hitch," I said, as she looked at me suspiciously.

"What?"

"You will have to go up there first in January, while I wrap up my affairs down here. I have worked for the company for fifteen years and will need to give them a month's notice. I will also have to move everything before I abandon the condo. You can live in a dormitory for the first semester, but we will be back living together by spring. I promise."

"I am not crazy about the idea of going up there without you, but I guess there is no other way," she said in a resigned tone.

I had over $400,000 in my 401(K) even after Jen had taken her share. I could make a hardship withdrawal of $100,000. That should be enough for her to get a four-year degree from a state school as an in-state resident.

My next problem was getting her mother's support. I had never spoken with her and was not sure how much they had been communicating or what Shmooky had said about me. I assumed that no matter how glowing her reports may have been, if she told her mother the truth about my age, there was no way she would ever approve. But I would need her mother's help keeping her up there once Shmooky realizes that I have lied to… uh, I mean, hoodwinked her. "Mrs. Wilenski?"

"Yes."

"This is Sam Russo."

"What are you doing to my daughter?"

"It's a long story."

"Well, you better start talking, you pervert, or I am calling the FBI."

I was on the phone with her for over two hours explaining how much I loved her daughter and how I had reluctantly concluded that it could never work. I told her that I would be sending a letter along with the college money. By the time I was finished, her mother assured me she would do everything she could to keep Shmooky from returning to Orlando and convince her to start college.

Once I received the money, the only thing left to do was to write the letter explaining my motives and hope that she will accept the fact that it is over. I agonized over every word for days leading up to Christmas. The letter would be mailed to her mother's address ahead of time and would be there waiting for her when she arrived back in that cold and dreary little town. Her mother would be there to comfort her when she read the letter and would explain that I did this because I love her. I finally settled on the following, although I realized while writing it that no words could adequately describe my anguish.

My Dearest Shmooky,   12/28/08

I hope that someday you will be able to read this letter without feeling anger and betrayal. I have agonized over what to do for several weeks and could not avoid the conclusion that I would ruin your life if I tried to hold on to you. I would rather do serious harm to myself than risk hurting you in the least. I want you to know that you have made the last four months the happiest of my life, and I will never forget you. I thought of trying, at the very least, to maintain our friendship, but I know that could never work. As I write this, I am longing to hold you, to touch you, to gaze into your beautiful face and see you smile. I never thought I could love anyone as deeply as I love you—a love so limitless that I will not allow my own desire to direct me. I am in intractable pain as I write this, which only confirms that the only way I can control my passion is to make the unalterable decision to never see or hear from you again.

I hope I have enclosed enough money to get you through school. It is yours on the condition that you obtain your degree. You have so much beauty, intelligence, and talent. Please do not let it go to waste.

Shmooky, you are not rejected. It is the circumstances that reject me. Please be assured that my desire for you is boundless, and as I write this I am desperately fighting the urge to abandon all I have, including my soul, to be with you again.

You will have difficult days ahead, but in your darkest moments, think of me and you will feel it. It is my spirit that will always be with you for the remainder of your days. You are, and always will be, my dearest, my passion, my love.

Sam

The trip to the airport was intolerable. Of course, not knowing the truth, Shmooky was in a jubilant mood. "I can't believe this, but I actually can't wait to see my mother. She will be so excited that I am finally going back to school. I think we will get along great from now on. Wait 'til she sees your picture," she said as she gently held onto my right arm as I drove. "She will be so jealous that I found a handsome and distinguished gentleman. She has been looking for someone like you since my dad died." She continued exuberantly, "I know a great neighborhood near campus where we can rent a house and be able to walk to football games next fall."

I smiled and nodded in agreement while desperately trying to hide my agony. It was like dealing with the death of a loved one, which in reality it was. Only a few more minutes, and it would be over. I would never see or hear from her again. The emptiness in my heart could never be refilled. I felt like living, breathing, walking death. What did I do to deserve this torture? Was there any possible alternative? It wouldn't be the first marriage with such a huge age difference, but it would be wrong nonetheless. I don't doubt she loves me, and when she reads my letter, she may even be devastated. She may never forget me as long as she lives. But she will live. She will fall in love again, marry and raise a family. She will get her degree and share her beautiful soul with the children she teaches. If I will have positively impacted her life, then I have finally accomplished something lasting. Failure would mean succumbing to my selfish desires and ruining the life of the woman I love. I won't do that, and it is killing me inside.

As we arrived at the gate, I felt overcome with nausea. Since she thought I would be joining her in five or six weeks, her emotions were under control. When I heard the dreaded announcement, final boarding for flight 347 to Cleveland, Shmooky jumped into my arms and kissed me deeply as I desperately fought back my tears. I heard a small child say to her mother, "Look at that, Mommy; she really loves her daddy." The child's mother grabbed her by the hand and pulled her quickly away as she looked back to give me the dirtiest of looks. I guess the world really isn't ready for Shmooky and me, and it doesn't help that she looks closer to sixteen than twenty-one. *This is the way it must end,* I thought, as we parted. I looked back once and as soon as I was out of her sight, burst into tears—tears I had not shed since my father's death seventeen years earlier.

With every bit of self control I could muster, I kept walking down the concourse desperately fighting the urge to run back to the gate. What started as controlled tears and sobs, quickly progressed into open and relentless weeping as my mind and body shut down with grief. I stared blankly ahead as passers-by gawked. Nothing registered in my mind except the monotonous reminder over the PA system from the Department of Homeland Security that the threat level was "orange" and to remain vigilant. It seemed to repeat over and over, and I couldn't help thinking of the absurdity of the warning as I was enduring the latest and most complete disaster in a lifetime full of them.

Unable to walk any further, I collapsed on a bench crying like a baby as others looked on. I was oblivious to the scene I had made until I heard, as if through a thick fog, the voice of a female security guard asking, "Sir, are you all right? Do you need a doctor? Sir, sir . . ." She gently touched my shoulder as I had been unresponsive. I looked up at her and saw genuine concern before noticing the crowd that had gathered. There must truly be something about the sight of a grown man crying as I saw despair in the faces of the onlookers as if they could feel my pain. All I could say was "I am sorry" and ran off as fast as I could.

Barging into the nearest men's room, I kicked open a stall door and threw my guts up with loud heaves, gasps and coughs. The crowded bathroom came to a standstill until I finally re-emerged. When I realized that I had such a large audience, all I could say was, "What!?" Embarrassed, they quickly looked away and went about their business.

I returned home and when the door shut behind me, I felt as if I was marooned in deep space. The cold silence overwhelmed my senses. I stood there for a moment and absorbed it all. There is no coming back from this. No eternal optimism can put a pretty face on this picture of slow, decomposing death. I immediately went to the bar and filled a tall highball glass with ice and what had to be a sextuple Johnny Walker Black. After downing it in about thirty seconds, I decided to skip the formality and drank the rest straight out of the bottle. I then walked into the kitchen and placed a photograph of Shmooky and me on the counter, along with a small gold crucifix my mother had given me. I opened the kitchen drawer, looked closely at my .40 Glock, and pondered my future.

Epilogue

And though we choose between reality and madness . . .
It's either sadness or euphoria
Summer, Highland Falls
                    —Billy Joel

Ultimately, I couldn't do it. To end it all now would be contrary to everything Shmooky did for me. It was four months of magic in a lifetime of disillusionment and disappointment, but it was magic nonetheless. She made me realize I have a life that is worth living and that I am a person that someone could fall in love with. Loving her gave my life meaning, and I doubt I will ever meet anyone like her. But maybe there is someone else out there who will be able to move me in a different way. How could I expect her to move on if I take the coward's way out? Maybe life is over for me in Orlando, but I may yet have a chance at redemption. I can still move to Vegas or call the guy with the phone books and ask him how to disappear without a trace. The point is, I have felt this way before and succeeding events proved that there is always hope.

That is the story of Shmooky and me. I hope you have had a few laughs along the way. I sure have. There is no need to have pity on me. The people I pity are those wretched souls who absorb all of life's shots without a smile and without laughing at the absurdity of it all. This unfortunate ending was inevitable, so I am not bitter. I could curse the cruelty of middle age: that era in a man's life when he has finally matured, reached his intellectual capacity and has become aware that he has acquired wisdom, only to see his body rapidly deteriorate as his mind starts its assured descent, having crossed the pinnacle. Or I could blame God for introducing me to my love, only to have her thirty-two years younger and, therefore, unattainable. None of that would serve any purpose. I had a good run and to know true love even for only four months is more than most people experience in a lifetime. It is those moments in time, no matter how brief, that make life worth living.

Sure, I was tempted to desperately hang on to her. She may have even stuck around for a few years before realizing her error. But I do love her and to attempt to keep her to fulfill my own needs would have been the height of selfishness. I couldn't do it. For once in my life, I did the right thing, no matter how much it hurt. I really am a lost soul. One of those hapless, lonely, middle-aged men: the kind you pass by every day without giving him a thought. In my case, someone did notice, and I am grateful. I have lived a deeply flawed life, but I can honestly say that I have done my semi-sober best to avoid the deliberate infliction of pain. If anyone did get hurt along the way, it was unintentional. It took me fifty-two years to realize that the only thing important in life is the love you give to the few people who matter and never delude yourself into thinking there are more than just a few. As for the rest of you, the only question I have is: Was it a good show?

Gordon Solie put on a good show and only his family knows what his last words were when he died of cancer on July 29, 2000. When I read of his death, I thought back to the lifetime of laughs he gave me. He took a ridiculous spectacle and made it worth watching. I hope you feel that way about this tale of woe. Since I have borrowed so many of his witticisms, I will end my story the way he always ended his show: "So long from the Sunshine State."